Christmas Clues

Christina Cooper

Other Books by Christina Cooper:

Follow Christina Cooper:

christinacooperunpublished.com

fb: Christina Cooper, Author

This book is dedicated to my dad- Santa Claus himself.

Chapter 1
The Letter

Noelle tucked her long, brown hair behind her ear as she carefully flipped the letter over in her hands. It took her a moment to catch her bearings. Seeing the lawyer's name on the return address gave her a sickening feeling in the pit of her stomach. It had been seven months since her mom passed away. What possibly could the law offices of Richard R. Reynolds want three weeks before Christmas? The realization of Christmas being so close gave her anxiety. Putting down the envelope, she grabbed a pumpkin spice candle and inhaled the sweet scent. She closed her green eyes and focused on her breathing.

Feeling a little more relaxed, she picked the letter up and read it, being sure to focus on each word so her thoughts wouldn't wander back to her mother. Confused by the entire situation and somewhat frustrated, Noelle picked up her phone and dialed her sister's number.

"Hello?"

"Hey, Libby. I was wondering if you got a letter from Mom's lawyer today," Noelle said. She bit her lower lip in anticipation of her sister's response.

"Yeah, I was just going to call you. What do you think they want?"

"I'm really not sure. I guess I was wondering the same."

"Do you think it's Mom's will?" Libby asked.

"I didn't think she had a will. It's been what, seven months since she passed- wouldn't all of that have been worked out by now? Besides, I figured that was what the money was that paid for the funeral."

"Yeah, you're right. That's weird."

"Unless..."

"Unless what?"

"Well, Christmas *was* Mom's favorite holiday. You don't think she pulled something off do you?"

"I guess that anything's possible. Did you read the date for the meeting? He wants us there tomorrow."

"Yeah, I saw that. How did he know we'd get the letter in time? This whole entire thing is weird. I don't like it."

"I hear you, but I'm going to be there. I just want to know what this is all about," Libby laughed.

"I guess I'll see you tomorrow then." Noelle hung up the phone and took another long breath before she stuffed the envelope into the drawer. She could feel the loneliness eating a hole in the pit of her stomach. The burning in the back of her eyes gave way to tears in no time. This was going to be her first Christmas with just her and her son, Levi.

Three years ago, Noelle had left her husband, James, and moved back home with her mother. She and her husband got along great when they were together, but that was the problem. He tended to prioritize work over his family, so they never were together. That became a bigger issue when work turned into him living in Japan for weeks at a time. She had gotten sick of trying to live her life isolated in a state nowhere near her family, when her husband wasn't even home most of the time anyway. She had written him a letter one night and packed her things and moved back to Michigan.

She hated the fact that she did it by letter, but she knew that if she was looking at him she wouldn't have been strong enough to go through with it. The truth was, she loved him. She had expected him to come chasing after her once he received the letter and then promise her that he'd change. She would agree and then he would whisk her off her feet and tell her how much he loved her and how sorry he was. She had quit waiting for that to happen two years ago. Instead, when he called, he would ask to speak to Levi and Noelle would turn her head, so her son wouldn't see that she was crying.

Noelle's mom, Grace, was actually her hero. Her name couldn't have been more fitting, she was Noelle's saving grace. Grace would tell her stories of her dad, who had died during the war when Noelle was just a little girl. Noelle was always comforted by her parents' love for each other. It gave her hope. Grace would tell her how they met, how he proposed, and then the stories of their first kiss and the wedding. Grace would laugh so hard at the memories. She was never bitter about his death. Never angry. Noelle couldn't relate. She was very angry with how her marriage played out. She and James had loved each other very much, or at least she thought they had. It got to the point that his business was going so well that he was in Japan for months at a time. She tried to tell him over and over again, but she never felt heard.

Neither one of them ever filed for divorce. She had thought about it a few times and she was sure he probably had too. But unless the other was trying to remarry, what was the point? The good part was, she still was on his health insurance plan. She wasn't sure if he forgot to take her off or if he just didn't mind that she was on it. Regardless, she was on it and that was okay with her.

Wiping her face, Noelle walked toward the door and watched for her son's school bus to arrive. She didn't want him to see her upset, he was just a little boy and Christmas was a magical time of year. Noelle didn't want to ruin it for him just because she was going to be feeling sad with it being just the two of them for the very first time. She thought of her favorite things that she would do for Christmas when she was a kid. She decided she was going to have to try new things out with Levi just so Christmas wouldn't feel so empty this year.

She felt her heart leap when the bus pulled up to the house. Watching her little boy jump off the last stair made her smile. She couldn't help but think of how much he reminded her of herself when she was little. She was an active little girl, often losing her sneakers or tearing her jeans. Her mom wouldn't know what to do with her, she was never sure if she should be frustrated or laughing.

Noelle smiled, remembering the day she tried to run the sprinkler in the middle of winter to make a frozen fountain. It was below zero the week they were on Christmas break and the water froze to Noelle's face and hands in no time. Moments later, the pipe burst. Noelle couldn't get the door open because the ice on her mittens were stuck to her hands. Her mom had a fit when she found out Noelle went outside in temps that cold. That was the day her mom began shutting off the water to the outside spicket. That disaster costed Grace a fortune. Noelle could see Levi doing such a thing.

Smiling, she quietly bent over and made a snowball. As soon as Levi came toward the house, she went to throw it at him, but she was too late. Levi had already had a snowball ready. He pegged his mom in the belly and then dove into the snow laughing. Noelle ran after him, grabbing a fistful of snow on the way. Carefully, she jumped in and put the snow down his jacket. Levi screamed with giggles. Together, bombing each other on the way, they ran for the safety of the home. Not realizing it, Noelle had momentarily forgotten about her sadness.

Once inside, Noelle looked at her son with his bright, rosy cheeks and smiled. He was starting to look more and more like his father. Levi had brown curls that peeked out of his hat. His big brown eyes flashed wildly with excitement anytime he could find mischief to get into. He was missing his two front teeth, but that didn't stop him from providing a big grin every chance he could. Noelle loves that smile. It's her favorite part of her son. He smiles so bright that his eyes shine. Nothing was more satisfying than seeing that.

Noelle thought about how the last time Levi saw James was three years ago. Half of his life. The thought made her sad. James called Levi regularly and he sent him gifts for every holiday and once in a blue moon just because. When he would call, Noelle would just have Levi answer the phone. She realized she hasn't really talked to him since she left him. It hurt too much for her to think about it. She hated that things ended the way they did, but she wasn't capable of sharing her husband with the rest of the world. She needed her guy to be home at least the majority of nights.

Noelle sat down at the table, contemplating what she was going to do about dinner. Her stomach was so cramped up from receiving that letter that she wasn't really in the mood to eat. She thought about it for a moment and decided that she had the perfect idea. When in doubt pizza is always a good choice.

"Levi, come help Momma out!" she exclaimed as she grabbed the pizza pan.

"What are we doing?" Levi asked.

"Making pizza!"

"Yum! Can I make a face with the pepperoni?"

"Of course!"

Together, Noelle and Levi pressed the crust into the pan. She smiled to herself as she remembered making pizza with her mom when she was a little girl. Noelle handed Levi a spoon and he spread the sauce carefully over the crust. Next came the cheese. Levi insisted that there was going to be a lot of cheese.

Finally, it was time for the mushrooms and pepperoni. He made a face with a great big smile. The mushrooms were the teeth and the ears. Joyfully, he clapped his hands as his mom put the pizza in the oven. He was very proud of his work.

After dinner and bath time, Noelle made sure Levi was tucked into the bed. Quietly, she grabbed the old photo albums from the bedroom and studied each page. Seeing her mom frozen in time, cancer free, caused her head to spin. She missed her mom more than anything. Her mom was her best friend. Noelle wished she had someone to talk to about the letter. Someone with sound advice who knew exactly what to say. Someone like her mom.

As soon as she sent Levi off to school the next morning, Noelle begrudgingly got ready to go to the lawyer's office. She had a knot in her stomach. She wanted to know what this was about and something inside of her said that her mom was behind all of it. She walked toward the office purposefully, though in reality all she wanted to do was turn around and go back home. She bit her lip as she forced the door open.

"Here goes nothing." She sighed as she walked in. Immediately she felt a smidgen of comfort upon seeing her sister already sitting there.

"Noelle, it's good to see you. Olivia, it's nice to see you too," Richard Reynolds said, smiling as he walked into the room.

"Libby," she corrected. "I'm only Olivia when I'm in trouble."

"I stand corrected. Libby, it's good to see you."

The sisters were staring at their mother's lawyer with anticipation. Neither one of them really knew what was going on, but neither of them wanted to be the first to ask. Discussing the finality of their mother's life was more than either of them was ready for.

Richard cleared his throat. "Well, I think we can get started," he said as he reached across his desk for a file with their mother's name on it.

Noelle glanced at Libby, who was staring at the file. It was a thick manila folder with their mother's name on the front and her initials on the tab. It was full of papers and things, though neither girl knew what any of those things were. As far as either of them knew, everything regarding their mom had been handled.

"I'll start off by saying, your mom was a wonderful woman and a dear friend of mine. I've known your mother for years. I just want you to know that it has been an honor and a privilege to not only work with her but both of you as well. That said, in working out your mother's final wishes, she was pretty demanding regarding some things. Please forgive me if some of these rules seem off-putting. They were what your mother wanted, and it is my job as her representative to carry out her final wishes the best way I possibly can-"

"-My mom was set in her ways, but I thought we were done with her will and everything," Noelle interrupted.

"Well, you only kind of were. Regarding her burial you girls did everything by the book.

All of that has been squared away and is settled. The one life insurance policy where both of you received a few thousand dollars a piece has been situated. However, your mother had a second insurance policy that I was forbidden to discuss until now..."

"Why now?" Libby asked with a confused look on her face.

"Christmas," Noelle muttered under her breath. Somehow, she feared this was her mom's intention. Her mother absolutely loved Christmas and it just kind of made sense to

Noelle that she would have one final Christmas wish. She squirmed in her seat waiting for Richard Reynolds to confirm her thoughts.

"Yes. It seems that your mother was a lover of Christmas," Richard agreed, a smile playing at his lips. "But there's a catch."

"Catch?" Libby asked.

"Yes. Your mother has a gift for each of you. However, it appears she became a little bored in her final days, so with the time she had she put together a little puzzle for you to solve," Richard looked at the girls apprehensively.

"Look, I know my mom meant well, but I don't think she realized how hard this is for us. Can't you just donate the money?" Noelle asked as she could feel her face burning with the hurt of thinking about her mom and the upcoming holidays.

"No. She knew you would ask that. She has a special gift for each one of you, including her grandchild; not just money, but an actual present. Her final wishes were that you two would solve this puzzle together. Let me add, it's more than just a single puzzle. From the sounds of things, it's quite elaborate," Richard said as he looked at them apologetically.

"Well, Noelle, if that's what mom wanted, we really have no choice."

"We always have a choice," Noelle muttered far less than amused.

"Yeah, but I can't just not do it. It wouldn't feel right. I'm in," Libby stated as she reached her hand out toward the attorney.

"I am not allowed to give you the clue until both of you agree to all of the terms and conditions."

"Terms and conditions?" Noelle asked, feeling even more flustered.

"Yeah. You may want to hear this before you decide," he added matter-of-factly.

"Okay? Let's hear it," Libby stated far more enthusiastically than Noelle felt.

Richard looked toward Noelle and raised his eyebrow as if he was waiting for her approval before he would continue. Noelle thought about her son and how this Christmas was going to be his first Christmas without his grandmother. What right did she have to take away a special gift for him, just because it hurt her so much to think about her mother being gone? That wouldn't be fair to anyone. Levi, Libby, even herself when she thought about it.

"I guess I'm in," Noelle replied with some hesitation in her voice.

Libby patted her on the leg. "I knew you'd come to your senses. There's no way we could just throw away mom's last gift to us. You wouldn't be able to forgive yourself for that down the road," she smiled warmly at her sister.

Libby had a point, Noelle thought. "Let's hear it," Noelle confirmed as she focused on the lawyer's face. Something about the look he had gave Noelle dread.

"The rules are as follows: Every clue must be accomplished before going to the next clue. If the clue doesn't get solved, you will have to wait until you solve it before going further. Days, months, years, doesn't matter. You only have until Christmas to solve the clues. Once Christmas has come and gone, the clues are null and void and then you will have to try again the following year. This is a collaborative effort. The four of you must work together to solve each clue-"

"-Four of us?" Libby asked, confused.

"Let me see… Here it is. Noelle White- Miller, Libby White, Levi Miller, and James Miller," the lawyer glanced up expectantly.

"James is in Tokyo. There's no way he's coming all the way here to solve a Christmas riddle," Noelle argued. "We can just do it without him."

"Actually, you can't. I'm not allowed to give you the first clue until all four of you are present in my office," Richard replied.

"What does it matter? It's a game!" Noelle argued.

"It's not just a game. It's a legally binding contract," Richard stated.

"What if he refuses?" Libby asked.

"The contract would be null and void. I can strongly encourage him to come though. I can send a certified letter requesting his presence. Typically, people comply," Richard suggested.

"There's no way. I'm not doing it," Noelle said as she stood up to leave.

"Noelle. Wait! This doesn't just affect you. You do realize this is my first Christmas without mom too, don't you? This affects all of us. You know that if we ask James, he will show up. He's like that. Truthfully, he's a nice guy, just happens to be a workaholic. Do you want me to ask him to come?"

"How about I send the letter out?" Richard offered.

"Look, fine. Libby, I'm only doing this for you and Levi. This isn't fair to me at all. If you want to have a letter sent, then do so. If you want to call him, fine. I'm not calling him though," Noelle crossed her arms over her chest. If this day wasn't hard already for her, it just got much worse with the thought of having to face James.

"Thank you!" Libby hugged her sister. "I'll keep it as easy as possible," she added. "Richard, if you could send the letter, I will call him. That way he hears it from both sides."

"Sounds like a plan. Let's meet here in my office in one week from today. That should give him enough time to fly in. How about at 10:00?"

"We'll be here," Libby said.

On the way to their cars, Noelle looked at her sister and shook her head. "I don't know how I'm going to pull this off, right before Christmas," she sighed.

"Noelle, I'll be here with you. You're not doing this by yourself. I promise, I will keep it the least awkward as possible. Scouts honor."

Noelle took a deep breath and nodded. "You're lucky I love you," she said as she smiled.

"Well, I love you too... Looks like this Christmas will be a family Christmas after all."

"We would have gotten together regardless. Why do we have to add James to the mix?"

"I meant with Mom too. She'll be present with us. It's almost exciting."

Noelle nodded. She understood what her sister was referring to. She couldn't deny that she felt a little curious about the whole thing as well. She just hated the idea of having James with them. It would feel so awkward.

Noelle went to bed that night thinking about her mom. As she tried to fall asleep, she couldn't shake the feeling that her mother was close to her, as if she were watching. She tossed and turned that night remembering all of the Christmas traditions they shared as a family as far back as she could possibly go. She wondered what tricks her mom had up her sleeve this time. She also thought about James and in thinking of him, the knot in her stomach grew. Would he actually show up next week? As much as she hated to admit it, a small part of her was very curious, perhaps even a little hopeful.

Chapter 2
The Clue

"Were you ever able to get ahold of James?" Noelle asked Libby quietly. She didn't want Levi to hear her as she sure didn't want to get his hopes up. Tokyo is a long way to fly in from with only a week's notice. It was the morning they were supposed to meet up at the lawyer's office. The snow had just started to fall, and Levi was out of school for his winter break.

"No. I left his secretary a message."

"What are we going to do? I mean what if he doesn't show?" Noelle sounded slightly anxious.

"Whoa, chill out, sis. We show up and see. If not, I'm sure mom's lawyer will have an idea on what to do next. Maybe he could subpoena him?"

"He's not a witness to a crime, there's no way he could legally court order him to come and fulfill a deceased woman's Christmas wish! Do you know how ridiculous that would sound to a judge?" Noelle was pacing the floor as she typically does when she's frustrated. Realizing it, she took a deep breath and inhaled the scent of her mom's favorite candle. The smell of pumpkin and cinnamon calmed her down enough for her to get her thoughts together.

"Okay, okay... It was just a thought. Look, either way I say we show up and see what's going on. Keep your head on, this is Mom, remember? She was always able to work some kind of magic or another in order to keep things running as planned. Do I need to remind you of the time when Santa Claus was sick, and we couldn't go to the mall and see him? Instead she took us to the grocery store with her and we ran into Santa driving a red car.

Mom said he wasn't dressed in his Santa suit because he was taking a day off from all that work."

"Yeah, I remember. We walked right up to him and started to tell him what we wanted for Christmas. The guy must have thought we were crazy!" Noelle laughed.

"Yeah, well he bought us each a candy bar and snapped a few photos with us," Libby smiled and shook her head. Their mom really was able to make magic happen in dire situations. "Noelle, no worries, it will all work out. Trust me. But let me let you go, we need to be there in a bit and I still have to get some clothes on."

"Okay. Thanks, Libby."

"Always!"

A little while later, Noelle pulled into the parking lot of Richard Reynolds' office. She took a deep breath and tried to calm herself down. She didn't want Levi to know that anything abnormal was going on. When he asked where they were going, she just said that she had to take care of some paperwork business.

Before leaving the car, Noelle took a long hard look at herself in the mirror. She tucked her long brown hair behind her ear and then pulled it out again. She smiled at herself making sure there was nothing on her teeth. Then she looked at her large green eyes. She absentmindedly wondered if she looked any older than she had three years ago. Part of her felt like she didn't look much different, but she definitely felt a lot older these days.

As her eyes started to well up, she took a deep breath and reminded herself that she was going to be okay, her mom must have known what she was doing. However, a part of her then wondered if she truly did. Her mom was quite sick in her final days. Biting her lower lip, Noelle told Levi that it was time to go in. She quietly reminded him to be on his best behavior, though truthfully, she knew she didn't have to. Levi was naturally well-behaved.

Together, Noelle and Levi walked in. The receptionist greeted them and walked them into the office. Libby was already in there, but James was nowhere to be seen. Immediately, Noelle's heart started to flip-flop. She smiled at Libby and instinctively rustled Levi's hair. She tried to look as if she were playing it cool, but the truth was, she was extremely nervous. She didn't know if she were slightly relieved, or highly disappointed.

Noelle looked at her sister and then at the lawyer expectantly. "What do we do now?" She asked.

"Well we are a little early," Libby reminded her.

"We'll give him a few," Richard agreed. Noelle noticed that this time around, Richard was wearing casual clothes instead of a suit like he was the last time. She couldn't help but notice just how handsome he was. He had a kind face and a strong build, unlike any other lawyer she's ever known before. His wife, Rachael, was one lucky woman. Noelle remembered when she felt that she was a lucky woman. She and James had truly been in love, but that was before he ever fell in love with his job.

"What are our options if he doesn't show?" Libby asked.

"Well, I'm not quite sure. I think we would have to try really hard to get him here. I guess if push comes to shove, I could see if I could pull some strings. Perhaps get him by phone or something…"

"That won't be necessary."

The three of them turned toward the door, when it was Levi to break the silence.

"Dad?" he asked. It had been three years since Levi saw his father, but he talked to him every week, usually several times a week. Levi recognized his father's voice in a heartbeat.

"Hey, kid! Oh, I've missed you so much!" With a quick leap Levi was up in his father's arms before Noelle could fully process what was going on.

"James, I assume?" Richard stood up and walked across the room to shake his hand. James smiled and with his free hand, shook Richard's. His right hand was holding his son.

Before Libby thought to do otherwise, she stood up and greeted James with a big bear hug. She had always loved her brother-in-law and even she felt the effects of their separation, though she would never admit it to Noelle of course.

Noelle felt the lump in her throat. It was so big that she had to open her mouth in order to catch her breath. She wasn't sure what to feel. Part of her was angry, but also relieved. Angry because he looked so good standing there. Better than she wanted to admit. Better than she could even remember. Relieved because she was going to be able to see what her mother was up to in her last days.

Noelle never stood up. She sat in her chair doing everything she could not to make eye contact with him. She hated the fact that he was standing there in the same room with her. He and his tussled dark hair, big brown eyes and five o'clock shadow. He was tall, his presence strong. Even worse, she could smell him standing there. The intoxicating smell of man, of strength. She opened her mouth to breathe, she refused to breathe out of her nose. She wanted nothing more but to be able to get this puzzle solved so she could go on with her life, alone. With Levi, of course, but definitely not with James.

"Noelle."

"James." The way he said her name gave her goosebumps. She decided she was cold and pulled her coat tightly against her. "So, let's get to the point of all this," Noelle said as she tried to refocus her brain.

Richard Reynolds nodded. "Just to fill you in James, Grace White left sort of a will for the four of you, however, it's a strange type of thing. She wants you to solve clues if you will, in order to get to the finish of the puzzle. At the end, she left each one of you a gift in addition to her life insurance policy."

"Why am I here? I am no longer a part of the family, nor do I need any insurance money. I definitely don't want to take anything from her daughters."

"Your guess is as good as ours," Noelle chimed in a little too eagerly.

"Apparently, Grace thought you were pretty special. She held you in high regard," Richard answered. "She was insistent that you were a part of this. What you do with the money and such is your choice. The rule is, you have to be physically present in order for anyone to get the will read to them. That means, the puzzle has to be solved with all four of you from start to finish."

"What about work?" James asked.

"The entire transaction is null and void if you leave," Richard gave him an apologetic look.

"James, we're only asking for a week or so. If that. I figured if we put our heads together, we can get this done pretty quickly. Please work it out so we can do this. This is our final gift from our mother," Libby said. She looked desperate.

"Okay. Yeah. I'll find a way to work it out."

"Yay! Daddy, you can sleep in my room!" Levi exclaimed gleefully.

"No, no. Daddy will get a hotel, I'm sure," Noelle interrupted.

"Well can I stay with him then?" Levi asked.

Noelle thought about it for a moment. It was the first time in three years that he has seen his father. How could she say no? On the flip side, she would be totally alone during the holiday season. All of the traditions she wanted to do with her son would be thrown out the window. She bit her lower lip anxiously.

"We'll see what happens," James said.

"So, should we get this thing started?" Libby asked with a smile on her face.

"Since this is a legal and binding document, I will need signatures from each of you stating that you understand the terms and conditions."

"Man, she was serious about this wasn't she?" Libby asked as she grabbed the pen.

Richard nodded his head. "Very serious."

Noelle signed her name next. James shifted Levi to his other arm and awkwardly signed his name. Levi took this as his cue to jump down and very carefully etch his name on the document, followed by Richard as the witness. Richard then grabbed an envelope out of the file.

"Ready?" he asked. The four of them nodded.

"Ready," Libby confirmed.

"Here is the first clue."

WITHOUT THE USE OF ELECTRONICS TO TAKE A LOOK
SANTA HAD 8 REINDEER NAMED IN THE BOOK
THE ONE WITH THE RED NOSE IS ACTING AS FIRST
FIND THE MIDDLE REINDEER NEAR A PLACE THAT QUENCHES YOUR THIRST
DRINK THE HOT COCOA AND HAVE SOME FUN
YOUR NEXT CLUE WILL NOT BE VISIBLE TO EVERYONE
REACHING INTO THE MOUTH IS WHAT YOU HAVE TO DO
LEVI SHOULD BE THE ONE TO FIND THE NEXT CLUE

"Well that doesn't sound too hard," Libby said, shrugging. "James you may get home a lot quicker than we expected!"

"I wouldn't count on it. Some of her clues were pretty complex, but that may have been my perspective. Perhaps they were some family secrets or something like that. Either way, I wouldn't count on it," Richard smiled and handed them the clue, so they wouldn't forget it. "Good luck and if you need anything, please feel free to ask. Hopefully I'll be seeing you soon," Richard said as he walked them to the door and opened it for them.

Together, the four of them headed out of his office and into the parking lot.

"So, do you just want me to take Levi and go get the next clue?" Noelle asked.

"You heard the rules, Noelle. Mom wanted the four of us to do this together."

"This one is simple. Besides, it's not like she's here to tell on us for not being together."

"I have a hunch she has eyes out," Libby stated. "I want to do it the way Mom wanted us to do it. All of us together. I'm serious."

"I think she's right. Your Mom had a plan, we might as well give her what she wanted. Besides, four heads are better than two," James stated.

"Fine. When do you want to do this?" Noelle looked at Libby and James expectantly.

"Do you mind if I get a room and change my clothes and then we can meet back up in a couple of hours?"

"Sounds like a plan!" Libby said. "We can meet at Noelle's house at 1:00. Noelle, I'm going to hold the clues, so I know you don't cheat."

"I won't cheat."

"I'm serious. Give me the clue."

"Fine. Here," Noelle rolled her eyes and handed her sister the clue.

"James, do you remember how to get to Noelle's?"

"How could I forget? I'll see you at one."

"Can I ride with Dad?" Levi asked, not letting go of his father since he first walked into the room.

James shrugged. "It's up to your mom, buddy."

"Yes, but you be good," Noelle agreed feeling a little disregarded, but appreciating the idea of a few minutes to process the day. "One o'clock," she confirmed.

Noelle walked into the house and finding herself exhausted from the mix of emotions, sank into the couch, kicking off her shoes a few moments later. She reminisced about the day she met James, the way he proposed to her, and then the day she left him. Thoughts flooded her brain as she remembered the good times along with the bad. She knew there wasn't really any seriously bad times, but the loneliness ate her up the most. She couldn't handle it. He was thousands of miles away and she was home raising a son with no family nearby. It didn't feel fair to her. She wondered if the marriage would have worked out if they had bought a house in this town, so when James was gone at least she would have family and friends nearby. That is a question she would never have an answer for. She left him. She was determined enough not to call him. She wanted him to chase her. He never did. Not once. It was over.

She was accepting of that idea in theory, but she wondered why seeing him for the first time since she left him made her feel so unsure. She felt confused. When she first saw him standing there it was like time stopped. She was breathless. Sitting there in his presence made her feel uncomfortable, even somewhat ashamed. What was wrong with her that she felt so unsure of herself? Noelle felt a headache coming on, so she reached into her purse to grab some aspirin. Realizing she had a little bit of time before everyone showed up, she decided to take advantage of the quiet and allowed herself to drift off for a few minutes.

Noelle awoke with a start. How long had she been sleeping? What time was it? Seeing that it was ten to one, she frantically got up and started to clean the house up a little bit. Realizing she had left dishes in the sink from the night before, she quickly tried to load the dishwasher and scrub the table at least before they showed up. While she slid across the linoleum floor to throw some papers in the garbage, she stubbed her toe on the corner of the wall. That's when she heard the knock on the door.

Noelle, with tears streaming down her cheeks rushed to unlock the deadbolt. There was no hiding her pain. Levi walked in first and gave her a funny look.

"Are you okay, Mom?"

"I'm fine, kiddo."

"You fell asleep, didn't you?" James was laughing.

Noelle shot him a look. "No. I just stubbed my toe," Noelle exclaimed.

"Yeah you did. You stubbed your toe because you were rushing because you fell asleep. Some things never change," James was enjoying this.

Noelle didn't find him amusing at all. She just shot him a look and opened the door, letting them in.

Libby walked in behind James and Levi. She had the clue in her hand. It was then that Noelle realized how important this was to her little sister. Noelle had been feeling sorry for herself for how much she missed their mom, but she never really thought about Libby. Noelle realized that as alone as she felt, she had a son to keep her company. Libby was by herself. No kids, no boyfriend, no mother, nothing. She had friends of course, but when it came to family, Noelle was really all Libby had left. For the first time that season, Noelle felt sorry for her sister instead of for herself. She had never meant to be selfish, but in her grief, it just never dawned on her. Noelle, as much as she didn't like this whole solving clues game, decided she would put forth a lot of effort for her sister's sake. That's the least she could do.

"Does anyone want anything to eat or anything?" Noelle asked, trying to remain pleasant, regardless of how bad James had irritated her. How did he know that she was sleeping, anyway? She found that to be rather frustrating, mostly because he was right.

"Me and Levi just ate," James said as he nonchalantly rubbed his stomach.

"Nope, I'm good. I had some soup at home," Libby replied.

"Oh," Noelle said.

"Make yourself something to eat. We'll wait," James smiled.

"I'm not hungry," Noelle lied.

"Yes, you are. You didn't eat yet because when you got home you took a nap on the couch," James reminded her.

"No, I didn't! I'm not hungry," She said that just as her stomach growled.

"See? Just get something and we will go," James stated.

"Just grab something Noelle, we have no idea how long this is going to take," Libby said.

"I'm fine!" Noelle insisted.

James shook his head. Libby rolled her eyes.

"Fine, I'll grab something if it makes you happy!" Her stomach growled again. Noelle grabbed the bread and James had already opened the fridge and pulled out the lunchmeat and the salad dressing. It irritated Noelle that he remembered how she liked to eat her sandwiches. It bothered her that he knew she was hungry and even more that he knew she was sleeping. She was frustrated that he knew so much about her, but never really cared that she left him. Noelle found herself wanting to tear up. She put her back toward them as she made her sandwich. She needed to get herself together and fast.

Taking a bite of her sandwich and simultaneously controlling her emotions, Noelle decided that it was time to take a look at the clue to get this show on the road.

"Libby, do you have that clue still?" Noelle asked, already knowing the answer.

"Yeah, I thought you'd never ask!" She pulled the clue out of her pocket and laid it on the counter.

**WITHOUT THE USE OF ELECTRONICS TO TAKE A LOOK
SANTA HAD 8 REINDEER NAMED IN THE BOOK
THE ONE WITH THE RED NOSE IS ACTING AS FIRST
FIND THE MIDDLE REINDEER NEAR A PLACE THAT QUENCHES YOUR THIRST
DRINK THE HOT COCOA AND HAVE SOME FUN
YOUR NEXT CLUE WILL NOT BE VISIBLE TO EVERYONE
REACHING INTO THE MOUTH IS WHAT YOU HAVE TO DO
LEVI SHOULD BE THE ONE TO FIND THE NEXT CLUE**

"Okay, so basically we just have to figure out where Santa's reindeer are located next to diners and coffee shops. Right?" Noelle asked, optimistically.

"I would assume so. What do you guys think?" Libby asked.

"That doesn't sound too bad. How many diners are there around here?" James asked as he pulled out his phone.

"No!" Libby exclaimed.

James' startled expression made Libby laugh.

"Sorry, I didn't mean to yell. It's just that the clue says no electronics."

"Oh. Right. You think she was serious?"

"Yeah. We're doing it EXACTLY the way mom wanted us to. It's in the rules."

"Okay, so this town's not that big, let's just take a ride to see if we can find different diners. Why don't we split up?" Noelle asked.

"No. It has to be the four of us together. Look, I know I sound like a stickler, but this is it. Mom's last words to us. I am really going to do this word for word the way she wanted us to," Libby protested.

"You're right. I'm sorry. Who wants to drive?" Noelle nodded her head remembering her dedication to make this right for Libby.

"Do you want to drive?" Libby offered, knowing that Noelle typically loved to be distracted when she's emotional. Libby knew she must be emotional having James there and everything. She figured she could give her sister this little token of appreciation.

"Okay." Noelle agreed happy with the task.

Together the four of them, sisters in the front guys in the back, went looking for reindeer next to coffee shops. After an hour and a half and about six different sets of reindeer the four became discouraged.

"I don't get it. We've read the clue a hundred times. None of the reindeer have a mouth on them that's open." Libby exclaimed feeling the frustration. "I thought this was going to be easy."

"Libs, it's Mom we're talking about. She was creative and fun. Nothing with her was simple."

"This whole time we've been looking for all of Santa's reindeer. Maybe it's just one?" James thought out loud more to himself than anything.

"Okay, so which one are we looking for?" Libby asked.

"Who's the middle one?"

"What were the reindeer's names?" Noelle asked reaching into her pocket for her phone and then stopping herself as she realized what she was doing.

"I don't know... I think Happy, Coment, Dixon, and Dumpy..." I don't really remember," Libby said with exasperation.

"No, it was more like Dancer, and Prancer, and Rudolph, and Nixon. I can't think of them all..." Noelle said.

"I have no idea. I haven't read that book in ages," James said.

"Those aren't it!" Levi laughed. "It's Dasher and Dancer and Prancer and Vixen. On Comet on Cupid on Donner and Blitzen!"

"There's no middle one. There's 8." Noelle added.

"Mom! Rudolph is first, remember!"

"Here, Levi. Say them again. I'll write them down, so we have the middle one," James offered.

"Levi, buddy, are you sure you're right on those. I thought one was Happy or Doc," Libby asked.

"We're talking about deer not dwarfs! I'm positive I'm right! Me and Grandma would read the book every time she babysat me! Trust me guys," Levi was in hysterics.

"Okay I got a pen. Say them again."

"Dasher and Dancer and Prancer and Vixen. Comet, Cupid, Donner, and Blitzen. Rudolph has to be first."

"Vixen is the reindeer we're looking for."

"How is this helpful?" Libby asked. "That doesn't negate the fact that all the reindeer's mouths were shut. We checked every coffee shop. It makes no sense."

"I don't know. I say we take a ride around again," James stated matter-of-factly.

"By the way, weren't we supposed to be drinking hot chocolate?" Noelle asked. "You said you wanted to do it just the way mom wanted."

"You're right. Who has the best hot chocolate in town?" Libby asked.

"That's easy. Hands down it's the igloo."

"Oh yes! They are the best. I almost forgot about that place! Let's go there!"

Noelle pulled into the parking lot of the igloo and together the four of them forgot about the puzzle as they were sipping on their hot chocolates. It was Levi to break the silence.

"Mom, look!" he said, pointing out the window.

"What are you looking at?" Noelle asked, following his gaze.

"That's funny, Mom, that's the name of the reindeer we're looking for."

"Vixen's? It's a restaurant. You don't think Mom would have thought to trick us like that do you?" Libby asked, inspired.

"Mom? Yeah, she would have, for sure."

"Guys look, there's a huge mouth eating spaghetti on the sign. Do you think that could be it?" James asked.

"It doesn't hurt to try," Noelle shrugged.

Together the four of them finished their hot chocolates and then ran across the street to Vixen's Restaurant. They looked at the big mouth on the sign and saw nothing. Disappointed they turned around to go back. Levi, however, wasn't convinced. From his viewpoint, looking up at the sign, he saw a little tear in the vinyl. He wondered if that could be the clue his grandma left behind.

"Mom. Check this out," he said.

"What?"

"The mouth has a little rip in it."

"Where? I don't see it."

"That's because you're big. Look up at it, Mom."

Noelle squatted down and looked up at the sign. Sure enough, in between the teeth, the sign had a small tear in it that only Levi would have noticed. "Here. Do you want to try and reach in and see if there's anything in there?" Noelle asked. "You have to do it very carefully, so we don't rip their sign more. I'm sure they wouldn't like that one bit."

"I'll be careful."

"James, can you boost Levi up so he can reach inside that tear?" Noelle asked.

"Absolutely! You ready buddy?" He held Levi up and quickly Levi reached just under the tear and pulled out a folded-up plastic bag with a paper inside it.

"I think I got it!" Levi said, happily.

"I think so too!"

"What are you guys doing to my sign?" Some guy came yelling out of the restaurant.

"Sorry!" The four of them apologized and waved as they hurried across the street.

The guy went and investigated the sign. He's tall too, so he never noticed the tiny tear that Levi pulled the clue out of or that Grace hid a clue in a year before.

As they ran toward the car, Noelle decided it would be best to park somewhere else to read the clue. She wanted to get as far away from the restaurant owner as quickly as possible.

"What does it say?" Libby asked impatiently.

"Hang on a second. I want to get this thing parked first." Noelle turned into a random parking lot, so she could focus on the clue.

YOU FOUND THE FIRST CLUE THIS I SEE
NOW THIS ONE IS FOR YOU OLDER THREE

**OFF THE CORNER ABOUT A HUNDRED FEET
FROM THE BIRD I LOVE AND MAIN STREET
YOU'LL FIND A STORE OR TWO OR THREE
THIS ONE'S QUAINT JUST WAIT AND SEE
INSIDE THE STORE YOU'LL HAVE TO SEARCH AND FIND
A PAIR OF MITTENS I LEFT BEHIND
ONCE YOU FIND THEM YOU'LL KNOW WHAT TO DO
IN ORDER TO GAIN ACCESS TO YOUR NEXT CLUE**

"What was your mom's favorite bird?" James asked curiously.

"I have no idea," Noelle answered.

"I guess we take a ride down Main Street?" Libby suggested.

Noelle pulled the car out of the parking lot. She glanced in the rearview mirror at her son and her ex-husband and felt the knot growing in her stomach. The two looked so peaceful, so handsome, sitting there next to each other. She bit her lower lip as she took a left onto Main Street.

She drove past the houses and small businesses. Past every corner and every street, they hunted for birds.

"There's one!" James exclaimed as he leaned forward, pointing toward Pigeon Drive.

He was inches from Noelle's ear. She could feel his warm breath hit her spine, sending shivers throughout her body. The smell of the cocoa he was drinking minutes before, in combination with his rugged cologne were dancing on the edge of her nose. Something inside her stomach tingled and she realized it had been three years since she's had a man that close to her. Three years, and he is the last man that was. She let out a slow even breath after realizing she had been holding hers. She closed her eyes trying to contain whatever sensation she was feeling, while at the same time denying any feelings at all. Libby must have caught her, from the corner of her eye, Noelle saw her smirk.

Noelle slowed the car down to turn. She had no idea if her mom liked pigeons or not, but this was the only option they saw. Driving a few blocks, Noelle realized there were no stores or anything that resembled a store within the vicinity of this area.

Apparently reading her mind, Libby piped in saying, "Maybe on the other side?" Noelle pulled into a random driveway and crossed Main Street to search the other side of Pigeon Drive when she realized there was no other side. Pigeon Drive started on the side they just drove on.

"This isn't the road," Noelle said.

"Why is this so hard?" Libby complained.

"Your mom was a genius!" James laughed.

At least he seemed to be having a good time, Noelle thought to herself glad that it wasn't as awkward as she envisioned it being. Part of her was sad that it wasn't. This was indeed their first time seeing each other let alone speaking to each other since she left him. He must have moved on already she assumed. The thought kind of struck a nerve with her and she found herself getting into a mood.

"What do we do now?" Noelle asked nobody specifically.

Nobody responded. It appeared they were all thinking the same thing. Noelle just drove. Up and down Main Street, she drove through each section of the neighborhoods, reading the street signs on every corner. Nothing.

"Wait. She said off the corner about a hundred feet. Instead of looking for a bird, lets look for weird stores." James thought of the idea.

With nothing to lose, Noelle turned every corner went around the block and turned on the next corner. Libby was jotting down each 'quaint' store she could think of and what street it was on, so they could revisit each store after naming every one of them. By the time they were done it was turning into nightfall. They found about 15 stores they would label as 'quaint'. It was Levi who figured out the method to his grandmother's madness.

"Momma, there's a bird." He pointed toward the chicken above the fast food restaurant.

"Chicken!" Libby exclaimed. "Duh! Mom's favorite fast food restaurant was this chicken place. She loved their chicken! I don't know why I didn't think of that! Good job, Levi!"

Noelle turned down the intersection that the chicken place was sitting on. Sure enough, there were three of the stores they had counted earlier. Libby scratched the rest off her list and they decided to check out those three.

"Which one would she consider quaint?" Noelle asked.

They all looked at the three stores to try and decide which store Grace would have labeled that way. The first one was an antique store, that looked like it was full of junk and clutter overflowing each aisle. The second was a thrift store that had a ton of used and new things mashed together for racks at a time. The third was a consignment shop, again overflowing with product jammed into racks. All three of them gave Noelle anxiety as she considered having to search them.

"Let's go," she announced after taking a deep breath.

"We can't. It's after 6. They're all closed," James said checking his watch.

"What now?" Libby asked.

"We can call it a night and start fresh in the morning," James seemed to be enjoying himself saying that. As much as Noelle thought he would be against this whole thing, he actually seemed to be having a great time. Almost as if he were excited.

Libby, though she started off being the most excited, seemed to be irritated with the idea. "I thought this was going to be a lot easier. We should have been done by now!" she stated.

"You're not having fun with this, Libs?" James laughed.

The way he said 'Libs' gave Noelle goosebumps again. She remembered when they first became serious and she introduced him to her family. He adopted the pet name for her, 'Libs' in almost no time. They were just like brother and sister. Noelle couldn't help but admit that she missed those days.

"Not really! It's hard."

"Think of it like this, this is Mom's last task for us. Ever. Have fun with it, somehow mom had this whole thing planned out before she passed. She must have spent a ton of time on it preparing and working out the fine details. It's her last wish for us," Noelle wiped a single tear that fell from her eye as she said it.

"You're right," Libby agreed with less reservation.

"Can I stay with dad?" Levi asked not concerned too much about the sentiment the sisters were experiencing.

Noelle caught James' eye as if to ask him if it was okay. She almost thought she saw a glimmer of sadness in it but then it was washed away with his smile. She shook the thought away, realizing that he could care less that she was gone and that his new woman was probably amazing and that she was just being stupid. "It's up to daddy," she said forcing herself to look away from James' intoxicating stare.

"Of course you can, Buddy!" James replied. Noelle could still feel his gaze on her. She refused to check to see if she was right.

Chapter 3
The Search

  Noelle couldn't sleep a wink that night. She tossed and turned the entire time remembering what it was like to be laying in James' arms. She remembered the night they got married. She remembered laying next to him, his big strong arms enveloping her as she snuggled into his warm body. The rise and fall of his chest as he breathed made her know beyond a shadow of a doubt that no matter what happened she would be safe as long as he was there with her. She thought to herself how long ago that seemed. She hadn't thought much about it recently, however, she realized she is definitely more alert at night since he hasn't been there. She realized she's definitely resorted to needing coffee more than she ever had in her past.
  Noelle flipped over. Her memories flooded her no matter which way she lay. She would close her eyes and end up back in time. She remembered their first Christmas. How special that day was. They had been together almost a year when he was standing under the mistletoe and as she puckered up to give him a big kiss, he dodged her, getting on one knee to propose. She got more than she bargained for, as her mother laughed and laughed. She enjoyed watching Noelle look silly, lips puckered up with nothing but snow falling on them. When she opened her eyes, she saw James with the ring. She gasped choking on her own spit or possibly a snowflake, nobody was really sure what she choked on. Her mother loved to tell that story.
  She thought about the time when she was going into labor with Levi. James was right there breathing with her, trying to coach her through the way their birthing teacher instructed him. Noelle tried to breathe but instead she would scream, and

James was right there, combing her hair or rubbing her back, handing her ice chips or anything else that she may have needed. He looked so panicked and yet calm at the same time. The way he was so careful with those scissors when he cut the umbilical cord. Noelle knew he would take care of their family no matter what.

No matter how hard she tried, the memories continued to flood her brain. She wanted more than anything to just sleep and get this little scavenger hunt thing done with. That way, life could go back to normal. However, she also wondered if normal is what she was really wanting. Part of her wondered if she even realized that she was lying to herself.

10:00 came and soon everyone was standing in her dining room. Noelle couldn't bare to look in the mirror again; she had purple bags accenting her green eyes. It wasn't appealing in the least. Noelle considered covering it up with makeup, but she wondered if there was even a point to it, anyone could see that her eyes were swollen and bloodshot. No amount of makeup could help with that. She decided to just let it be and hopefully the coffee would help make her look or feel more alert.

"Did you have fun last night?" Noelle asked as she gave her son a big squeeze. She basked in the feeling of endorphins as they surged through her body. At least that was one good thing she could look forward to, her son always had the best hugs.

"Yeah, me and Daddy watched wrestling and he showed me some new moves!" Swallowing, Noelle's face turned bright red. She cursed her brain for being slightly jealous.

"Well that sounds fun!" she stated a little too enthusiastically.

"Mom, it was! Dad can show you."

"No, no, no, that's quite alright," Noelle said, blushing even more.

Libby started to laugh. "Are you sure Noelle, Levi said it was fun! I think you could use some fun," she jabbed at her sister.

Noelle shot her a look. "I think it's time we get ready to go."

"I think it is too," James cut in.

The four of them piled up into Noelle's car. "Do you guys want to split up for each store or do you want to do them one at a time?" She asked, grateful for the change in subject.

"Splitting up seems logical, but mom didn't intend for it to be that way," Libby stated.

"I agree. Besides, I would have no idea what type of mittens we would be looking for," James added.

"So, we do each store in order?" Noelle asked.

"Did mom ever even wear mittens?" Libby asked as she read the clue again.

"Your guess is as good as mine," Noelle replied. "Can you read the clue out loud again?"

YOU FOUND THE FIRST CLUE THIS I SEE
NOW THIS ONE IS FOR YOU OLDER THREE
OFF THE CORNER ABOUT A HUNDRED FEET
FROM THE BIRD I LOVE AND MAIN STREET
YOU'LL FIND A STORE OR TWO OR THREE
THIS ONE'S QUAINT JUST WAIT AND SEE
INSIDE THE STORE YOU'LL HAVE TO SEARCH AND FIND
A PAIR OF MITTENS I LEFT BEHIND
ONCE YOU FIND THEM YOU'LL KNOW WHAT TO DO
IN ORDER TO GAIN ACCESS TO YOUR NEXT CLUE

"Who would have guessed mom to be so poetic?" Libby asked after handing Noelle the clue. James reached for it next. The three adults passed it to each other, all of them seeming to understand the clue, but not really sure what to make out of it, since Grace stumped them a few times already.

"Mom was really creative. Remember how she used to make our Halloween costumes?" Noelle laughed at the memory. "One year I was a tree. That costume was awesome!"

"Yeah, I remember that. But I didn't know she was a writer too," Libby trailed off. "She was good at pretty much everything."

"Yeah. Mom was something, that's for sure," Noelle smiled remembering her. She really did miss her mom, but she was grateful she was there in spirit.

"Okay, on this journey together, let's get this thing going," James' suggestion snapped everyone back to their mission.

"How about each adult takes a store and searches out mittens. Levi can go with anyone he wants to and help. Once the mittens are all in a pile, we, together, will go through each store and each pair of mittens. That way, we are working together, but we're getting a head start at the same time. Do you think that's acceptable?" Noelle looked toward the group expectantly.

"It's not going to work. Mom specifically said work together. Something will go wrong. Let's just tackle each store one-by-one until we find them. That way, we're complying with the plan."

"Not that I mind or anything, but I think this clue is going to take a lot longer than we expect. I'm with Libby. I think we should tackle each store one-by-one as your mom wanted. Who's to say that somebody's not watching and puts the mittens out when we're together? The lawyer seemed to allude to that to me," James said.

"You're right. Why don't we check out each store and get a feel for which one feels 'quaint'. That way, there's no need to go in order if we don't have to," Noelle suggested.

"I think that's a good idea," Libby replied.

The four of them were on a mission. They decided to stop at the antique store first.

Together, they walked in. Immediately they noticed the piles of stuff that was sitting on makeshift shelves and sitting on the floor.

"This feels like a fire hazard," Libby muttered under her breath.

"All antique stores are like this," Noelle replied. Boxes of things were sitting out on old desks that still had inkwells sitting on them. Tin lunch boxes from the 70's were scattered about. Jars of marbles, hats with wide brims and old tea kettles were strewn throughout. There was an old lady with grey whiskers standing at the desk who looked like she could have owned every single thing in the store, who greeted them.

They kindly smiled at her when Levi broke the silence. "This place smells quaint, that's for sure."

The adults had to stifle their laughter as they walked past the front desk and into the cluttered store. Each section of the store was separated with a number. Apparently, each number was how they figured who contributed what to the store. Certain booths had sales, certain ones did not. All of them were equally as cluttered. The place looked like a mouse's fantasy land.

"How are we ever going to find mittens in here?" It was James who asked the question that each of them wanted to know.

Noelle shook her head exasperated by the idea. She stepped over a toy fire truck as she walked toward an old world map. She remembered having one like that in her class when she was in elementary school. Beyond that, she saw about three Tickle Me Elmo's and about five Mr. Potato Heads. Noelle thought about growing up with those toys and smiled at the memory.

She walked deeper into the store with Libby and James on her heels. Both of them continuously reminding Levi not to touch a thing. There were glass ducks sitting on a shelf next to wooden owls. Old door handles were in a box next to a big jar of buttons. Noelle would try and remember to look for mittens, but she kept getting sidetracked with all her childhood toys.

"I had that phone!" She exclaimed as she pointed to a see-through plastic phone.

"That's a phone?" Levi asked, surprised. "Why does it have a wire hanging out of it?" He asked.

"That's what phones used to look like, Buddy," James replied with a laugh.

"Any mittens?" Noelle asked the rest of the team.

"None." They replied in unison.

They continued on their journey through the store. Old Milton Bradley games stacked the shelves one by one, puzzles, flags that didn't have enough stars on them, and political buttons were scattered about in glass shelving. Every now and then they would come across an article of old clothing hanging up on a coat rack or something, but it all looked like it was from the 1800's and none of them mittens.

After about thirty minutes and a few sneezes later, the group decided this was likely not the quaint store they were looking for. They walked out, eager to get a breath of the fresh, crisp, cool air outside. Levi let out another sneeze before they walked into the thrift store.

Some stuff was older and some was new, a lot of it was irregular or only slightly used. Noelle thought someone who wanted to fulfill old wedding wives tales could come to this store. She felt like it had everything, including blue, borrowed, new or used. With much less dust, the group took a walk through on a mission to find mittens.

Feeling a lot less crowded, they could relax a little as they searched the shelves and the racks. "It'd be a lot easier if we knew exactly what we were looking for," James said as he pulled his hands through his hair. Noelle grinned to herself. She remembered how he used to do that when he would pay the taxes. He would be concentrating on them and not realize he was doing it. That would be when she would walk up to him and rub his shoulders. Instinctively she started toward him, but she stopped herself remembering that it was probably inappropriate to do so. Libby shot her a funny look. Noelle just shrugged it off and continued her search.

"I don't remember Mom ever wearing mittens!" Libby announced to the group about 15 minutes later.

They had pretty much searched the store, when they decided to try the consignment shop. Somehow Noelle had a strange feeling that the mittens weren't going to be found in the consignment shop. She regretted the thoughts that they were going to be found in the antique store, but as much as she wanted to find them, she didn't want to go digging through that place again. She kept the feeling to herself as they headed back into the cold and toward the final store.

After another thirty minutes of searching through people's used clothing, Levi broke the silence.

"I'm hungry!" He said.

Noelle looked at him and could tell he was bored. She patted him on the back at the same time James patted him on the back too. Immediately she felt the electricity travel up her arm leaving her goosebumps in its trail. His hand was strong and very warm. She wasn't sure if it were her imagination or not, but he didn't seem to move it once he realized his hand was touching hers. She recoiled almost immediately. *Almost.* She may have lingered for a split second. She wasn't truly sure.

James' eyes met hers. She pulled her gaze away and looked at their son. Their beautiful son, an object of their love years ago. She shook the thought from her head and then bent down, asking him if he could wait another ten minutes before they got some food. He nodded. He grabbed his mom's hand and his dad's hand and finished his walk through the store. Noelle could feel James' electricity bouncing off her skin through her son's hand. She took a deep breath as she felt her hand clam up in Levi's.

Ten minutes and no mittens later, the group decided lunch was a necessity. Wanting to stay in the vicinity of the three stores, they decided to eat their mom's favorite chicken. They took a booth near the window and the four of them ate a family box with biscuits and sides included.

Noelle made Levi's plate and as she grabbed hers, James was already holding up a chicken breast and dropping it onto her plate. She realized, just like old time's, he served her first. Noelle bit her lower lip as he scooped the potatoes onto her plate, instinctively. It was like he didn't even think about it. She smiled at him and started to eat.

Libby grabbed her food after kicking her sister under the table. Noelle shot her a look and Libby smiled defiantly.

"So James, how does it feel to be back in Michigan after all these years?" Libby asked him. Noelle went to kick her sister and instead kicked Levi.

"Ow," He exclaimed, rubbing his leg.

"Oh, I'm sorry, kiddo, Momma was just stretching her leg," Noelle said as she glared at Libby.

"I didn't realize how much I've missed it here, to be honest," James said as he glanced at Noelle.

Noelle took a bite of her chicken and didn't say anything. Libby took it upon herself to continue prying.

"How does it feel to see Levi and Noelle after all this time. I bet it's nice isn't it?" she smiled slyly. Noelle went to kick her again. She missed kicking the table. She almost spilled her pop in the process.

"Is it me or are these booths pretty small?" She asked in her embarrassment.

"Actually, I think it's just you," Libby said, enjoying her sister's discomfort. "James you were saying?"

"I mean yeah, it's great. I can't believe how much I've missed them," He replied, sipping his pop.

"So are you still working all those hours in Tokyo?" Libby pried.

"Actually, yeah. When Noelle left, I buried myself in my work. I mean what else could I do? I had nothing left but my job," James glanced toward Noelle and then back at Libby.

Noelle's face reddened. She bit her lower lip nervously. Suddenly her chicken didn't taste nearly as good.

"So, are you seeing anyone?" Libby asked a few moments later.

Noelle's eyes shot up. At first she was going to punch her sister, or desperately try to change the subject, but a part of her wanted to hear the answer.

"No. Not at all. I just put my house up for sale and buried myself in my job. I've been staying at a little apartment in Tokyo. I haven't even been to the states in about a year or so. I hate staying there in our house. It's too empty," He glanced at Noelle and then down toward his plate grabbing a bite. He decided it was probably time to change the subject.

"So, what about you, Libby? Anyone special in your life?"

"Nope, I'm happily single. I can't stand being tied down. I refuse to date unless a guy meets every quality on my list."

"She actually carries the list with her," Noelle laughed.

"I do. I keep it with me every where I go."

"So, what's on your list?" James asked taking the bait.

"He's got to be good-looking. He has to have ambition. He has to have dreams and want to follow them all the while wanting me to follow my dreams. He has to be creative. He has to be good with children. He has to be independent."

"She pretty much wants a dog," Noelle laughed.

Libby nodded. "Pretty much."

"Doesn't sound too bad. You'll find him one day."

"One day," Libby agreed.

"What about you, Noelle. Are you seeing anyone?" James asked it in a way that caught her off-guard. His eyes pierced hers and she found herself mesmerized in his causing her to be speechless.

"Are you kidding? She's been waiting for three years for you to come back and sweep her off her feet. After she left you, she swore you were going to come chasing after her, begging her back and promising you wouldn't be gone all the time."

"That's not true!" Noelle said in a way that didn't even convince herself.

James took another bite of his food not saying anything at all. The entire table was silent until Levi asked for another biscuit with honey on it. Noelle grabbed the biscuit and James grabbed the honey. The two locked eyes as he poured the honey onto the biscuit.

"Uh, that's a lot of honey," Libby said, as the honey poured off the biscuit and onto the table. James quickly caught the honey with his other hand, handing the biscuit and a napkin to Levi. Noelle blushed. James wiped his fingers off as he shook his head.

"I think I'll pay for this and we can get searching for those mittens," James said as he met Noelle's gaze again.

Noelle nodded. Her heart was pounding against her ribs. Libby was giggling as if she had no care in the world.

Moments later the three of them walked back into the antique store. The elderly woman at the front desk was still there, this time she was reading a newspaper.

"You're back," she smiled.

"We're on a mission," Libby replied.

"I see, anything particular?"

"We're looking for my mom's lost mittens."

"Was she a vendor here?"

"No."

"Then I doubt they're here, but you can take a look. What do they look like?"

"None of us know."

The old lady gave them a funny look. Noelle smiled and shrugged. Libby went to try and explain, but then she closed her mouth, she wasn't quite sure how to explain it.

"Thank you," James said as he lead the way away from the register. The little old lady smiled and nodded.

Together, again, they all wandered the store. Nothing that even resembled their mother was in the store. Their mom was artistic yet somehow kind of classy. She was smart, but funny. Their mom didn't keep things, she liked big open spaces and neatness. If she ever did have clutter it was more artistic like art supplies, drawings, papers, things like that. None of this even came close to fitting their mom. Not at all.

"Something here has to remind you of her. There's got to be a hint of some type or something," James said.

"Not that I see," Noelle stated, suddenly feeling very claustrophobic in that store.

After another 15 minutes go bye, Libby shouted from the back corner of the store.

"Noelle, what about here?"

Quickly, Noelle made her way to Libby's voice.

"Graceland?" Noelle said out loud. The entire booth was packed full of Elvis memorabilia.

"Yeah, she loved Elvis. Besides her name was Grace! Maybe that's a clue?" Libby exclaimed.

Noelle shrugged. She supposed it couldn't hurt. Sitting on top of an old Elvis wig were a pair of pink mittens with the words 'Grace' embroidered on them.

"Are these it?" James asked, holding them up.

"I don't know, maybe?" Noelle replied.

What do we do with them?" Libby asked.

Noelle grabbed the mittens and put them on her hands. She remembered a story their mom told them about the day she met Elvis.

"Wait! Libby, didn't she say she shook his hand and never wanted to wash her mittens after that?"

"Oh yeah! I remember that story! She said that was one of the best days of her life. She met the king of rock and roll!"

With the gloves on, Noelle walked to a life-sized statue of Elvis and shook his hand. Out of his sleeve dropped a piece of paper. Noelle quickly bent down to get it at the same time James did. The two bashed their heads together.

"Ow!" Noelle grabbed her head, wincing.

"Oh my goodness, I'm so sorry. Here," James grabbed the back of Noelle's head and held his palm up to her forehead, pressing into it to help alleviate the pain. He removed his hand to take a peek and then softly kissed her on the spot that hurt. Noelle felt the fireworks exploding around them. She would never admit that though, and just shook it off as if her head was pounding from the pain.

James stood there caressing Noelle's head. His eyes were searching her soul. His lips were tender, and he couldn't help but wince in pain as he smelled the familiar scent of her shampoo dancing with his nose. Levi walked up to them and he instinctively backed off.

"Did you find the next clue?" he asked.

"I think so," Noelle still feeling her head throbbing but also feeling the lightning flash down her spine, bent over to show Levi the piece of paper. "Should we read it?"

Levi sneezed. "Let's read it in the car," he suggested.

Everyone laughed.

"I'll meet you guys there. I think I'm going to buy these mittens," Libby said as she turned them over in her hand.

Once everyone had their place in the car, Noelle decided to open the slip of paper to see what the next clue was. It read:

GOOD JOB YOU GUYS YOU PASSED THIS TEST
THIS DAY WAS LONG YOU MAY GO REST
BUT WAIT TOGETHER YOU FOUR MUST BE
THE ENTIRE TIME YOU'RE DOING CLUE GAMES WITH ME
WITH ALL OF YOU A SLEEPOVER NIGHT
GET ALONG TOGETHER DON'T YOU DARE FIGHT
DON'T TRY TO SNEAK OFF THIS I WOULD SEE
I HAVE EYES ON YOU EACH PLACE YOU'LL BE
SPEAKING OF EYES THIS GAME IS FUN
TOMORROW MORNING RISES THE SUN
IF THERE'S SNOW MAKE A SNOWMAN OR TWO
THEN CLIMB LEVI'S TREE AND FIND YOUR NEXT CLUE

50

Chapter 4
The Sleepover

"A sleepover?" Noelle sighed in midair, obviously contesting the situation to her mother, but because her mom was not there, she was speaking to no one in particular.

"This sounds like fun!" Levi exclaimed with glee.

Noelle looked in the rearview mirror. Levi's dark curls were bouncing up and down with the excitement from his body. James ran his fingers over the dark scruff on his face. His brown eyes appeared to be happy, though contemplative. She glanced toward her sister who caught her eye. She regretted glancing her way as soon as she noticed Libby raising her eyebrows up and down and nodding toward James. Noelle rolled her eyes and she would have jabbed, or smacked Libby had James and Levi not been in the car.

"Can Dad sleep in my room?" Levi asked as he kicked his foot against the seat.

"I'm not sure Buddy, it sounds like Granny Grace wanted all *four* of us to be sleeping together. Isn't that what it sounds like to you, Noelle?" Libby had a huge grin on her face. She was having way too much fun playing match maker.

Noelle thought to herself that she was definitely going to have to get revenge, but not at this current moment. She didn't want to make a big presentation in front of her son or James. "I'm not really sure what she wanted. I wasn't here when she wrote the clues," Noelle stated hastily.

"It says we must stay together. I'd hate to have this game messed up because you refuse to have fun," Libby replied.

"Yay! Me, Aunt Libby, Daddy, and Momma all get to sleep together!"

"Levi, don't say it like that," Noelle corrected. Her voice was already drowned out with James' and Levi's chatter. It sounded like the two were making big plans for the night.

Noelle glanced at her sister who had a smirk on her lips. She rolled her eyes and continued to drive. Hearing her ex in the back laughing with their son gave Noelle a giggly feeling in the pit of her stomach; though of course, that could just be gas from the chicken they ate earlier. If one were to ask Noelle, that's exactly what that feeling was.

They pulled into the driveway and the four of them agreed to meet back at Noelle's house in two hours. James had to check out of the motel and grab his luggage if he were going to have to stay there and Libby had to pack some clothes. Noelle wanted a few minutes to "freshen up". Everyone knew that she really just needed some time to process the plans of that night and possibly clean up the house a little bit, not that the house wasn't already clean enough.

As she walked in to the front room, it dawned on her that Christmas was in less than two weeks and she didn't have her Christmas tree up yet. She had forgotten all about it. Suddenly guilt washed over her. Her mother never forgot to decorate or put the tree up. She wondered what kind of mother she was, not even remembering the details of the most important holiday of the year. She started to feel sorry for her son. Noelle took a deep breath and then decided that the best way to amend this is to have the four of them put the tree up later this evening during the sleepover.

Feeling the anxiety from the idea of a sleepover with her ex-husband and sometimes irritating younger sister, Noelle grabbed her mom's pumpkin spice candle and immediately calmed herself down. Just smelling her mother's favorite array of flavors and spices made her mom feel more present, as if she wasn't present enough this week. She glanced at the ceiling, grateful to be on this voyage that her mother put together for them, but also curious as to what her mom felt she was proving by her strange tasks and rules. Noelle smelled the candle again and then decided to grab the tree from the spare room upstairs.

Having to shuffle underneath some boxes of decorations, bags of old clothes, and a variety of other things, it took Noelle a moment before she was able to find the box that had the tree in it. Once she recognized the box, she felt like she had to move mountains before she could even get to it. In doing so, Noelle came across some of the old clothing her mom had worn when Noelle and Libby were just children. Noelle remembered her mom wearing some of the shirts when she was cooking, or painting, some of them were what mom considered to be her 'church shirts'. Most of them were covered with paint splatters or Easter egg dye and things like that. Their mom didn't dress up often and it was normal to see her in paint covered clothing. Their mom was very creative, not very graceful at all, and always getting into things.

Immediately, it hit her! She knew exactly what she was going to do for Libby for Christmas this year. She was so excited she could hardly stand it. Maybe this Christmas wouldn't be so terrible after all. In fact, their mom was more present than Noelle ever thought possible. With tears streaming down her cheeks, Noelle found some of her mom's most favorite articles of clothing and put them in a separate box in the corner of the room so she wouldn't forget where it was. Once she was done with that, she decided she better hurry to get the tree downstairs. It was almost time for everyone to arrive.

Noelle had to move several boxes and not realizing how heavy they were, Noelle found herself feeling overwhelmed but also determined. She couldn't help but wonder how in the world the tree ever made it up the stairs to begin with. She was always at work when her mom took the decorations down. There must have been a trick that she wasn't aware of. Either that, or their mom was a lot stronger than she ever gave her credit for. Noelle pushed and pulled and was only making it toward the stairs, inches at a time.

A few grunts and groans and a ton of pushing and shoving later, Noelle was able to get the massive box to the top of the stairs. She heard the faint knock on the door. "It's open!" She yelled at the top of her lungs. She heard the voices of her son and James. She pushed the box a little further, this time it was balancing on the top stair. Noelle didn't think this through. With the weight of the box and her being on the stairs, when she pushed it the final time, the box slid down the stairs with Noelle tumbling behind.

The box slid across the floor. Noelle landed half way on the box and the rest of her was crumpled up on the bottom of the stairs. James came running to her rescue.

"Noelle, are you okay?! Why didn't you wait for me, I would have helped you!" He kicked the box out of the way, scooped her up into his arms and gently placed her on the couch.

Noelle was in hysterics she was laughing so hard. Her embarrassment of falling must have struck her funny bone, because she couldn't stop laughing. Tears were streaming down her cheeks. If she felt any pain at all no one would have realized it. Her laughter was contagious because both James and Levi caught the giggles.

"Seriously, Noelle, are you okay? Do you hurt?" His face was just above hers. She focused on his beautiful features. His square jaw, perfect teeth, the tassel of hair that fell on his forehead, the big brown eyes that she first fell in love with the minute she met him, his sturdy frame, and the biceps that were protruding from his shirt. She noticed everything, especially the familiarity of him. Her heart pounded against her ribs. He was just inches away from her. She felt his warm breath dance across her lips. Her laughter subsided.

"I'm okay," she managed. She felt awkward, maybe a little melancholy. She wondered what happened in her marriage that she was so quick to leave and why he didn't come after her.

"Are you in pain?" he asked.

Noelle could hear Levi in the background. It was obvious he was worried about her. "I'm a little sore, but I think it's mostly my ego," she admitted. She locked eyes with him. The pounding in her chest was magnified with the feeling of him still holding onto her. Silence. Butterflies.

She swore she felt him move closer. His eyes half shut. She took a deep breath anticipating his mouth against hers, when the front door opened. Just like that it was done. He was standing, wiping his hands on his jeans and then pulling his hands through his hair.

"What's going on?" Libby asked, apparently sensing some kind of tension.

"Nothing unusual. Your sister just took a dive down the stairs. Just making sure she didn't break any bones or anything," James let out a laugh. Noelle could tell that it was forced, at least she thought it was.

"How did you manage to fall down the stairs?" Libby asked, not worried in the least about whether or not Noelle needed to go to the hospital or anything.

"I was trying to bring down the Christmas tree. I have no idea how mom managed to do it every year. That box is half broke and heavy as all get out!" Noelle explained.

"She didn't. She brought the Christmas tree down section by section. That is why the bottom of the tree is always on top.

Mom would bring the base and the bottom branches down and then she would go back up and get the rest. You didn't know that?" Libby laughed.

"No. But that makes a lot more sense than what I was trying to do!" Noelle exclaimed.

"Besides, it's about time you get the tree up. What's taken you so long?"

"I just haven't been in the Christmas spirit," Noelle admitted.

"Well, I guess that answers the questions on what we're going to be doing tonight. We need to get this tree up and decorated!"

"Mom, can I help put the Christmas tree up?" Levi asked.

"Of course you can."

Together, the four of them started to work on the tree. Libby put Christmas music on the radio and was jamming to Andy Williams, James started with the base and attached each branch, Noelle and Levi worked on fluffing the branches out. Pretty soon the tree was ready to be decorated.

Each person took turns picking out ornaments and arranging them perfectly on the tree. Their mom had collected ornaments from all around the world. Each one had a story of its own. From big clear glass bulbs to goldfish, to peacocks, pink elephants, little clowns, Santa Claus and elves, to pianos and pickles each ornament had some kind of representation of the White family Christmas.

"This one we can't put up yet," Noelle said, holding the bumpy pickle in the palms of her hands.

"Noelle, do you remember how hard we would compete to find that thing?"

"Why were you looking for a pickle?" James asked curiously.

"Your family never did that?" Noelle laughed. "I guess it's an old tradition. The pickle gets hung while the kids are in bed. The first one to find it gets an extra present."

"Really? Can we do that Mom? Can we find the pickle ornament?" Levi asked, intrigued by the thought of an extra gift.

"I'm sure we can," Noelle replied, smiling at the memory of her and Libby getting into arguments over who spotted the pickle first. If Noelle remembered correctly, Libby never won. Libby probably remembers it a different way though.

When they were just about finished with all of the decorations, Levi turned off the living room light. The four stood there admiring the tree in its glory.

"I have to hand it to you gals, I never thought I would like a white Christmas tree before, but after it's all said and done, it's amazing!"

"White trees are my favorite. They feel peaceful," Noelle admitted.

"It reminds me of snow," Libby added.

"Mom refused any other type of tree. She loved that the trees went with our last name. She always loved having a 'White Christmas.' That was even her favorite Christmas song!"

"Do you remember when we needed a tree so bad because the cat broke ours? Mom searched high and low for her white Christmas tree. When she couldn't find it, she finally bought a huge green one and then she spray painted the entire tree! I will never forget the look on Dad's face when Mom came out of the garage, choking on the paint fumes, full of paint, and satisfied because she finally had the entire tree turned white," Libby laughed at the memory.

"Yes, do you know how many cans of paint that took her to accomplish?" Noelle shook her head. "She was one obstinate woman!" she said, laughing at the memory.

"Runs in the family," James said quietly as he winked toward Noelle.

Noelle blushed.

"I just can't wait for the presents to be under there!" Levi shouted as he hopped up and down pointing toward the bottom of the tree.

Everyone laughed.

"I guess I can start cooking dinner. I'm starving. Does anyone have any requests?" For some reason Noelle was hoping that James would ask for something specific. The one thing she knew for sure was that he used to love her cooking. She coyly wondered if his new woman cooked as well as she. She desperately hoped not.

"Will you make chicken pot pies?" Libby asked.

Noelle felt her face flush. It wasn't James, but she offered, so she agreed. In fact, much to her disappointment James never said a word.

"Does that sound okay for everyone?" Noelle asked, trying to recover from her disappointment. Crickets. "Chicken pot pies it is," Noelle muttered under her breath, not able to hide her frustration very well.

Noelle went to the kitchen and started boiling some broth and cutting up vegetables. The chicken breasts were already seasoned and cooking with the broth. This wasn't going to take her too long. She had premade crusts in the fridge, so once the chicken was cooked all the way through she could put the whole meal together.

"You're trying to hard," Libby said.

Noelle jumped, dropping the knife on the floor right by her foot. "You scared the mess out of me! I almost cut my toe off!" she exclaimed.

"Yeah, but you didn't. Besides, you're wearing shoes."

"What do you mean I'm trying to hard?"

"With James. It's obvious how you feel. Relax. He's still in love with you."

"Are you kidding me? First of all, I don't feel anything..."

"...Right..."

"Second of all, he's nowhere close to in love with me. If he were why didn't he come after me? Why didn't he even try to save our marriage?"

"Maybe, just maybe he couldn't. You hated his job. What was he supposed to do? Quit? He owns the company. Japan is where his work is. Perhaps he just wanted you to be happy. Remember, Noelle, you're the one that left him. Have you ever considered that he could be as heartbroken as you were?"

"No. That doesn't even make sense. If he were, he would have contacted me three years ago!"

"Not if he knew he couldn't fix it. You do realize, you guys are still married, right? Noelle, he kept you on his insurance policies. That wasn't by mistake. The man loves you. It's obvious."

"I don't think so. He probably forgot that I was on it. I bet he's with another woman."

"Oh, stop feeling sorry for yourself. Besides, could you blame him? His wife left him three years ago. I bet he drowns himself in work. Yeah, he may date once in a while, I'm sure. I would too if I were him. Either way, he's here now. Today. You need to stop the pity party and talk to him. Ask him why he didn't chase after you. Tell him how you feel, Noelle. Do it before it's too late."

"I feel nothing."

"Liar. Tell him."

"I can't. Mom said she doesn't want arguments. So you may want to leave the kitchen too. She has spies watching us, the clue said so."

"Your loss, Noelle. If it were me, I would jump at the chance. Just look at him, he's gorgeous and even better, he's an awesome dad. A woman would be lucky to pick him up and like I said, if he were dating, I wouldn't blame him in the least."

"Okay, I get it. You don't need to rub it in."

"Talk to him."

"I can't!"

"That's why I requested this meal. You need to see exactly what you look like!"

"Carrots?"

"No, not carrots you dork. Chicken. A great big chicken!"

Noelle rolled her eyes. She didn't look like a chicken. She wondered to herself what really was stopping her from having a good heart-to-heart with James. Was she a chicken? She finished cutting up the carrots and started mixing the broth as she made gravy. She poured the meal into the bottom crust and then put the top crust over it. She pinched the crusts together and drew a big 'L' for Levi on the pie. She then carefully put it in the oven. It wouldn't be long and the whole house would be smelling like the savory dinner pastry.

Noelle washed her hands and decided that she could also make popcorn balls. That was her favorite treat when she and Libby would have sleepovers during the holidays. She checked the cupboards to make sure she had the ingredients and sure enough in no time at all she was forming red and green popcorn balls for dessert. Cooking was one thing Noelle really loved to do. She was good at it, too. It gave her peace to be able to provide nourishment for her family. That was one thing she excelled at as a mother. She could never compete with her mom regarding craftiness, creativity, or anything like that, but she was hands down the best cook of the family. She even dreamed of opening her own restaurant one day.

The four of them sat at the table together as they got ready to eat. Noelle served everyone the pot pie and then had the popcorn balls sitting in the middle of the table, for whoever wanted them when they were done. They looked pretty, like ornaments sitting there. After a few scrapes of the forks, the entire table became really quiet. Noticing the silence, Noelle glanced up to find everyone was staring at her.

"What's the matter?" She asked, feeling insecure.

"Noelle, this is the best meal I've had in years!" Libby stated.

"Oh. Thanks," she sheepishly replied.

"She's not kidding Noey, this is so good!" James agreed.

Noelle bit her bottom lip. The last time he called her, 'Noey' was when they were still married. "Thank you," she said.

"Ahem," Libby cleared her throat and shot Noelle a look.

"Bless you," Noelle said, shooting her sister a look back.

"Momma, can I have some more?" Levi asked.

"You finished your plate already?"

"It was good!"

Everyone laughed. Noelle scooped some more of the pot pie onto his plate. By the time dinner was over, there was only a small piece of the pot pie left. Noelle was surprised. She just whipped the recipe up out of her head. She didn't expect them to love it as much as they did. She was glad about it though.

"So what's the plan for tonight?" Libby asked, breaking the silence.

"What do you guys think?"

Everyone shook their heads.

"We can do popcorn balls and Christmas movies," Noelle suggested.

They all agreed.

"James, can you help me move the furniture out of the way. My back is a little strained from falling earlier."

"I bet it is! Of course I'll help. Where do you want me to go with them?"

"I guess just push it off to the side. Libs, do you want to grab the sleeping bags out of the closet? I should have at least three in there, maybe four."

"Got it."

"Levi, how about you grab your doggy pillow and then you can already have it for bed."

"Okay, Mama."

The four of them were working as a team just as Grace wanted. Noelle was surprised at how easy this was. She was expecting total awkwardness. She was grateful for James not to make it weird. He was always really easy going, but she didn't expect it to be this easy. By the time the night was over, the four of them were sound asleep on the living room floor.

Chapter Five
Snowmen and Trees

Noelle woke up first thing in the morning and seeing that everyone else was still asleep, she took it upon herself to start cooking breakfast. She scrambled some eggs, fried the sausage and started some blueberry pancakes.

"Smells good," James startled her.

Noelle jumped. "Man, this is becoming a habit," she laughed nervously. That's when she noticed him, strong looking in his tee-shirt and pajama bottoms. She couldn't help but remember what he looked like without the pajamas and she silently scolded her brain for being juvenile.

"Sorry, I didn't mean to scare you," he said.

"No, I've just been a little out of sorts I guess," she replied.

"Is it weird me being here?"

"Actually no, not at all. Why does it feel weird to you?"

"No. It feels right. Like it's supposed to."

Noelle pondered those words for a moment. She couldn't help but wonder what he meant by that. She wanted to ask him, but she didn't want to feel dumb either. She decided to let it go.

"James, I was wondering…"

"Mom, are you making pancakes?!" Levi interrupted.

"I sure am!" she hugged her son and ruffled his hair.

James scooped him up and gave him a big hug. Levi cuddled into his father's arms and started to go on and on about their day making a snow man.

James glanced at Noelle, wanting her to finish what she was saying, but the moment was gone.

Noelle finished cooking the pancakes and by that time, Libby had gotten up and had taken her place at the table. James and Levi were next to each other, James pouring syrup on Levi's pancakes. Everyone ate until they were full. Noelle and Libby loaded the dishwasher while James was in the shower. Levi had already gotten dressed and was getting his snowsuit on. He was ready to get on with his day. Levi loved looking for clues.

James walked out of the bathroom as he was pulling his shirt over his head. Noelle couldn't help but stare. She decided that James must have been working out in the three years they've been apart. Either that, or she took for granted what he had to offer. He was absolutely beautiful. It took everything inside of her not to run into his arms and melt right on the spot. Instead, she bit her lower lip and watched him as Levi jumped into his arms again. Noelle would never admit thinking that Levi was lucky, but then again, she didn't appear to be in the mood to admit a lot of things. The only person she was fooling was herself.

Libby, clearing her throat not so subtly again, broke Noelle from her trance. She gave Noelle a strange look and then announced that she too, was going to take a shower. Noelle nodded and handed her a towel. Libby was in the bathroom singing Christmas tunes the entire time. Noelle smiled, remembering that Libby always sang in the shower. For everything that Noelle could cook, Libby could sing. Grace used to brag that Libby had a voice of angels. Noelle was never jealous of her sister's voice, she was never the type to be brave enough to sing in front of people anyway. Libby was. Instead, Noelle would sit on the floor when they were kids and request songs for Libby to sing. The two would do this for hours. Noelle smiled at the memories.

Tired, Noelle sat down on the kitchen chair to relax for a moment. Feeling a little achy from the fall the day before, she tried to stretch her shoulders and back. Seeing her in discomfort, James set down Levi and gently moved Noelle's hair off of her neck, massaging her neck and shoulders. Noelle immediately felt the heat from his hands on her spine and the goosebumps popped up from head to toe.

"Relax," he whispered.

Noelle felt his hands tenderly smoothing out the tension at the base of her head. His thumbs rubbing over the nape of her neck and then slowly his hands moved over her shoulders and then dug a little deeper into her shoulder blades. Noelle forgot what it was like to have a massage. It was as if years of stress and anxiety left her in just a moment of time. His hands traveled up to her head and behind her ears as he gently rubbed each pressure point.

"Man, your muscles are tight. Is all this from your fall yesterday? Maybe you should have went to the hospital," James said. "When was the last time you had a massage?" he asked.

"Three years," she said. Her answer was truthful and flat. Noelle felt James stop for a moment. It was as if he had to process what she had said. Slowly, he began to gain momentum and her muscles were putty in his hands again.

"Three years, really?" he asked quietly.

"Really," she replied sheepishly. She wasn't sure why she was embarrassed. She assumed he had probably dated a lot in those years, but she didn't. Not really anyway. She had a few 'dinner dates' as she called them, but she never really cared much about them. She kind of went as a favor to her mom and sister. The truth was, Noelle hasn't even kissed anyone since she started seeing James years ago. When she left him, she wasn't really interested in anyone else. She just wanted a good, healthy marriage.

"That surprises me," James admitted.

Noelle wanted to ask him why it surprised him, but she decided some things were better left unsaid. Besides, she was enjoying the massage and didn't want to hear the intimate details of James' love life. She could see herself getting into a fit of jealous rage and that just wouldn't help anything at all.

"You should probably get dressed," James interrupted her thoughts. "We have a clue to solve."

Noelle took a deep breath and nodded. He was right, they needed to get on with their day. Reluctantly, she got up and stretched her back.

"Thanks," she said as she walked toward her room to grab her clothes.

"Anytime," James replied.

The way he said it almost sounded promising. She shook her head, shutting the door behind her. Overcome with emotion, Noelle sat on the bed waiting for the moment to pass. She wondered what she was doing. She had this man, her ex-husband, husband even, sitting in her kitchen, rubbing on her neck and shoulders, and she felt totally vulnerable. She thought how childish she was, she was the one to leave him, not the other way around. But then she thought about the fact that he never came after her. Not a single time. She found herself feeling defeated.

Taking a deep breath, she pushed the thoughts out of her brain and threw some clothes on. She realized she needed to snap out of this feeling and just finish the game. As soon as it was over, James would be leaving, probably back to Tokyo, and she would be alone with her son again. As unsettling as the thought was, it was also comfortable.

She decided to put her clothes on in her bedroom instead of waiting for the bathroom to free up. She would take a shower at night, there was no way she was going outside with wet hair anyway. Noelle had a difficult time deciding on what to wear, which was surprising because she was only going outside to build a snowman or two. She found herself gazing at herself in the mirror. She would suck her stomach in and then puff it out. She tried to decide if she looked good or just like a mom. She shook her head wondering why she was worried about it anyway. There was really no need to try and impress anyone.

Noelle decided on a purple sweater to go with her jeans. Simple, casual, and yet kind of cute. She pulled her long, brown hair into a ponytail and then threw on some eyeliner and mascara. Eyeliner and mascara were a must for every day, even if she was only going to the mailbox. That was the only thing that made her feel somewhat alive. Looking closer at herself in the mirror, she noticed a little blemish near her nose. She picked at that for a moment but then got really frustrated that she could see an age spot on her forehead. She was only 33, but compared to her younger sister and James, she felt like she looked 55. She took a deep breath and decided to present herself even if it was only to guarantee her son a good Christmas.

Noelle walked out of the bedroom and Levi was already dressed and ready to hit the snow. She quickly brushed her teeth and then grabbed the clue from her purse so they could make sure they followed it correctly. The only thing she really remembered about it was the snowmen. She read the clue to the rest of the team.

> **GOOD JOB YOU GUYS YOU PASSED THIS TEST**
> **THIS DAY WAS LONG YOU MAY GO REST**
> **BUT WAIT TOGETHER YOU FOUR MUST BE**
> **THE ENTIRE TIME YOU'RE DOING CLUE GAMES WITH ME**
> **WITH ALL OF YOU A SLEEPOVER NIGHT**
> **GET ALONG TOGETHER DON'T YOU DARE FIGHT**
> **DON'T TRY TO SNEAK OFF THIS I WOULD SEE**

**I HAVE EYES ON YOU EACH PLACE YOU'LL BE
SPEAKING OF EYES THIS GAME IS FUN
TOMORROW MORNING RISES THE SUN
IF THERE'S SNOW MAKE A SNOWMAN OR TWO
THEN CLIMB LEVI'S TREE AND FIND YOUR NEXT CLUE**

"This clue sounds easy enough," Libby said.

"I wouldn't plan on it. Each of them so far has sounded easy. I don't know the catch to this one, but I'm kind of scared to find out," Noelle replied, laughing.

"Well, to be honest, I'm kind of excited. This is actually kind of fun to me," James admitted.

"Me too!" Levi agreed. "Come on, let's build a snowman!"

Levi had no reservations running straight into the snow. He made a snowball and started pushing it through the snow to make it bigger and bigger. When it got quite big, James helped him to push it to make the base. They did the same for the medium sized ball and then again for the smaller one. In the meanwhile, Libby and Noelle were searching the garage area and the yard for some type of way to decorate the snow guy. That's when Noelle had a great idea.

"We can use the Mr. Potato head parts!"

"That would be awesome!" Libby agreed.

After a few minutes of searching, Noelle found a big box full of Mr. Potato head pieces. She then found an old mop that she could easily pull apart and they used that for hair for the snow woman. After a little more searching, Libby was able to find an old jacket of Levi's and a facemask and even some goggles. The women were laughing when they rejoined the guys with all of their findings.

"What's so funny?" James asked.

"Just wait and see," Noelle giggled.

"Can you make a couple more of those snow people? It didn't take you guys very long and we have enough stuff to dress them."

Intrigued, the guys agreed. In no time at all, there were four snow people built. Noelle and Libby had fun decorating them up. The biggest snowman was wearing a flannel shirt and was carrying an old shovel. He was wearing glasses and a scarf. The snow woman had the mop hair and big red lips. She was wearing a tankini bathing suit with goggles and flippers. One of the snow children was wearing a jacket and he had big ears with a goofy grin. Then there was a younger snow child who was wearing a bib and had two big teeth.

James and Levi were cracking up after seeing what Noelle and Libby did to the snow people. James pulled out his cell phone and snapped some pictures of the snow people, before shoving the phone back into his pocket. Almost immediately Libby pulled Noelle aside.

"Did you see that?" she asked.

"What?"

"James' wallpaper on his phone."

"No. Why?"

"I'm not sure, but I think it was a picture of the two of you together."

"Yeah right. It was probably him and whatever woman he is seeing."

"You might be right, but I don't think so. I could have sworn I've seen that picture before. I think it's you two."

Noelle thought about it for a minute. It didn't even make sense that James would still be carrying around a photograph of the two of them together after being apart for three years. Regardless if it made sense or not, something in the pit of her stomach longed for it to be true, but she couldn't shake the feeling of jealousy that said that it wasn't.

"Okay," James interrupted Noelle's thoughts. "We made the snowmen, so it says to find the clue in Levi's tree. Which tree is his?"

"I'm not sure. Levi, which tree did granny consider to be yours?" Noelle glanced around the yard. Their area was full of old Oak trees. They had a couple of maple trees in the back as well.

"I don't know," Levi shrugged. He was playing around the snow people, he didn't seem to care about trees or the like.

"Did it have anything to do with eyes?" Libby asked.

"Why eyes? What are you talking about?" Noelle questioned her.

"Mom's clue said, 'speaking of eyes, this game is fun.' That doesn't really go together. I just wondered if she was rhyming something or if that was a clue within a clue."

"Ahh, Good point."

"Let me hear that clue again," James said.

GOOD JOB YOU GUYS YOU PASSED THIS TEST
THIS DAY WAS LONG YOU MAY GO REST
BUT WAIT TOGETHER YOU FOUR MUST BE
THE ENTIRE TIME YOU'RE DOING CLUE GAMES WITH ME
WITH ALL OF YOU A SLEEPOVER NIGHT
GET ALONG TOGETHER DON'T YOU DARE FIGHT
DON'T TRY TO SNEAK OFF THIS I WOULD SEE
I HAVE EYES ON YOU EACH PLACE YOU'LL BE
SPEAKING OF EYES THIS GAME IS FUN
TOMORROW MORNING RISES THE SUN
IF THERE'S SNOW MAKE A SNOWMAN OR TWO
THEN CLIMB LEVI'S TREE AND FIND YOUR NEXT CLUE

"Levi, Buddy. What tree was gran talking about? Did you ever climb a tree with her?"

"All of them that I could," Levi replied.

The adults looked around the yard. "All we really know is that we have to climb a tree. Let's start with the ones with low branches that we can climb on," Noelle recommended.

"Levi, are you sure you didn't have a special tree?"

"I don't think so."

"I guess we survey the area and see what trees we could actually climb."

"The easiest ones equal four. Six if you get a little more complex."

"Why would she call it Levi's tree?" Libby asked.

"I don't know. I guess we'll find out," Noelle replied.

"Are there any memories with any of these trees and Levi?" James asked.

"Not that I can think of. I guess we can start with the tree that has the swing on it. Maybe she's counting that one."

James licked his lips and jumped up onto the branch that contained the rope for the tire swing. It was cold outside, and he was glad he was wearing boots and gloves. The tree bark was somewhat slippery. It was easy to look with all the leaves gone. James wasn't exactly sure what he was looking for, but he definitely knew the leaves would have made it much more difficult. Finding nothing he jumped off the tree and shook his head. "Nothing that I saw."

"Okay, which one is next?"

"How about the one by Levi's sandbox?"

"Okay," James hopped up onto the lowest branch. This tree being a lot smaller was much easier to search around for a clue. He even looked in the trees for possible holes made by animals and even nests. He didn't see anything. He glanced down at the girls and shook his head.

When James made his way off the tree, he decided he might as well go to the next closest one which was near the shed where Levi's outside toys were stored. It was a little more difficult for James to get up this tree because the tree was a lot bigger. After a few jumps, he made his way up the branches and looked around for a clue. The girls gave him suggestions pointing at a few possible places, but each one came up empty. James even shimmied across one of the branches that reached out near the house to see if it was on that, but the answer was no.

Feeling frustrated, Noelle tried to think of the tree her mom was talking about. The clue wasn't that easy and she was starting to wonder if they were misinterpreting something. The last tree that was feasible to climb was near Levi's window. Something in Noelle's head realized they weren't going to find it there, either. She didn't say this to the rest of the team though, just in case she was wrong.

James climbed the tree. Noelle could tell that he was getting warn out climbing them, but he didn't let that slow him down. He definitely was a good spirited guy. She wondered more and more as this clue game carried on, why she ever left him to begin with.

James climbed up other branches, looking for the clue but finding nothing. On his way back down, his foot slipped, and Noelle let out a little screech. Catching his boot on some of the bark, while holding on for dear life, James was able to steady himself. Libby laughed out of nervousness and James joined her.

"Are you okay?" Noelle asked after she gained some composure.

"Yeah, just a little slip," he replied.

"See what happened there? You could have lost him, and he would have never known how deeply in love with him you are.

I'm telling you, Noelle, life is precious, you need to talk to him," Libby jabbed her.

Noelle didn't want to admit that Libby was right. Instead she just shrugged, "He was fine."

"Mmmhmmm. Next time he may not be."

Once James landed safely on the ground, Noelle called Levi to them again. "Levi, is there any other tree that you can think of?"

"Not outside," Levi replied.

"What do you mean not outside? Do you have a tree inside?"

"The one that I painted."

"How are we supposed to climb that?" Libby asked.

"It's felt. He has little felt guys that can climb a ladder to the top of the tree." Noelle wasn't sure why she didn't think of that to begin with.

"You mean I did all that work for nothing?" James asked, laughing.

"I'm not really sure yet, but I think we can find out. Let's go check." Noelle lead them to the family tree that Levi put together. It was full of pictures of his family, and little felt pieces that stuck to the tree to represent pets, hobbies, and things like that. Sure enough at the top of the tree was some eyeglasses.

"I think I get the speaking of eyes in the clue part," Noelle wondered out loud.

Levi grabbed a little felt man and climbed the tree toward the random glasses that was stuck to the top branches. He lifted them up and there was a little string poking out of the felt that was sitting behind the glasses. Noelle pulled the string until it couldn't pull anymore. She then pulled the tree off the wall and looking behind it noticed the note stuck to the string that she was just pulling on.

"Mom, it's the clue!" Levi screeched.
"It looks like it," Noelle agreed.
"Can I read it?"
"Sure you can."
"It says..."

LOOK AT THIS YOU DID IT AGAIN
I SMILE AS I PICTURE NOELLE'S BIG GRIN
LARGE EYES THAT ARE GREEN AND HAIR SO BROWN
I REMEMBER HER BEAUTY IN HER WEDDING GOWN
JAMES NOW ITS YOUR TURN
REMEMBER THE PASSION THE WAY IT WOULD BURN
WHEN YOU SAW MY DAUGHTER WALKING DOWN THE AISLE
I WANT YOU TO SCULPT HER AND THAT BEAUTIFUL SMILE
TAKE YOUR TIME WITH EVERY DETAIL AND LINE
THE REST OF YOU ENCOURAGE HIM HE'S DOING FINE
WHEN YOU'RE DONE THIS IS WHAT YOU DO
TAKE IT TO THE DENTIST WITH THE FUNNY SHOE
HE'S THE ONE THAT MADE HER SMILE GLINT
ALSO THE ONE WITH YOUR NEXT HINT

"Uh, she wants me to do what?" James laughed.

"You heard the woman, you have to sculpt my sister," Libby replied.

"Sculpt her with what?" James asked.

"James, you're creative, you invent and draw marketing concepts and design graphics for gaming, a simple sculpture of my sister shouldn't be too hard!"

"Can you not be so eager to call me simple?" Noelle piped in.

"I didn't mean that *you're* simple, just that it should be simple for James to be able to sculpt you."

"Why, he's not a sculptor," Noelle stated matter-of-factly. "What does design concepts have to do with sculpting? And my original question was, sculpt her with what?"

"Daddy, you could sculpt her with snow, like we did the snowmen," Levi suggested.

"Or you could use ice," Libby said.

"Or you could just pretend to have sculpted me and just find the guy with the shoe," Noelle recommended.

"No!" Libby and James said at the same time.

"We're doing this the right way, Noelle."

Noelle sighed. She wasn't sure she liked this idea very much. She felt like she was being put on display and that was not her idea of fun.

"I could use clay, I suppose," James thought about it. That was pretty much what he did at work when he was trying to sell an idea to a major company. "I've never really tried to replicate a human before, but I've made lots of monsters. I'm sure I could probably figure something out," he was talking more to himself than to the others.

"A monster? Really? I'm feeling attacked. First simple, then a monster. Oh, and by the way, why me?" Noelle was starting to become frustrated, perhaps more embarrassed.

"Noelle, who knows, that's what mom wanted. Chill out, okay?" Libby snapped.

"Jeez," Noelle sighed. She thought about having to pose for James and her face reddened. The thought of him having to study her so closely made her very self-conscious.

"Well, Buddy, do you have any clay?" James asked Levi as he ignored the sisters.

"No. I don't think so," Levi replied.

"I do," Noelle offered. "I have a ton of it."

Everyone had a surprised expression as they looked at her.

"What? I got bored sitting here, so I started taking some pottery classes," she said.

"Well let's get started then!" James clapped his hands together and rubbed them eagerly. He was an artist, he could handle this.

Noelle blushed. "Now?" she asked.

"I'm with Noelle, I think she should probably take a hot bath and slip into something a little more comfortable," Libby grinned at Noelle and gave her a quick wink.

Noelle blushed, knowing what her sister was thinking. She knew that Libby wanted to rekindle the flame between her and James. The problem was, Noelle knew that would never happen again. James wasn't interested. She was sure on that, if he were, he would have been back for her a long time ago. The thought caused her anxiety to rise. She was going to have to pose for him to sculpt her, the whole time knowing that he likely has another woman, 10 times prettier than she. Noelle felt ridiculous even having to follow through with such a thing. It also made her very self-conscious. She felt like an old maid. She felt her face flush harder with the thought.

"How about I cook us up a nice lunch and then we can get to it? That way, it's out of the way and we won't have to stop later for me to cook." Noelle bit her bottom lip hoping they couldn't tell that she was trying to get out of it, or at least postpone her humiliation for a while.

"Yes, that sounds great! Then we can get straight to work," James agreed.

"What will you and Levi be doing when we're doing this?" Noelle asked.

"We'll probably play a game. Does that sound like fun?"

"Yes, can we play the smelly game? Or maybe the toilet one?" Levi was excited.

"He's like his dad; I was the same way, the grosser it was, the better," James laughed.

Noelle nodded. The truth was, Levi was a lot like his father. He was creative and smart, and the boy was charming too. He got his good looks from his father. Noelle wondered what ways Levi was like her. She smiled remembering how Levi stopped some kids from teasing another at school, in that sense he was a lot like her. He was also very mischievous, she was always that way too. She felt her heart flutter when she realized Levi was a perfect combination of her and James. *Together*. She shook the romance out of her brain, seeing that she was going to have to start dating soon, or perhaps get really involved in yoga. She was driving herself insane.

"We'll probably be able to play both. Your mom and dad will probably be a little while," Libby replied, pulling Noelle from her thoughts.

Mom *and* dad. Together. An item. Noelle grinned. She liked the idea that she and James were linked together like that. It has been a long time since she heard unity regarding she and James. If she were to be honest, it felt really nice. She shook her head. She was being dumb. That was something that would never happen again. They were separated. Apart. Taking a deep breath and absentmindedly grabbing her mother's candle to get the warmth of her mom's favorite smell, Noelle wiped her hands on her jeans and then pulled her hair back into a ponytail. Then, after washing her hands, she started to pull food out of the refrigerator. It was time for her to get a grip on things. Cooking was how she did just that.

Noelle thought simple would be sufficient on that cold, wintery day. She decided on making grilled cheese sandwiches and tomato soup. She decided that was the perfect comfort food. She smiled as she started to prepare the meal. Before long, Levi came running through the kitchen.

"Mom do I smell grilled cheese?"

"Yep. Grilled cheese it is!"

"Mom, you're the best mom ever! That's my favorite!" Levi licked his lips and rubbed his tummy excitedly.

"Well thank you!" Noelle smiled. She decided food was another area where Levi was like she was. They both had a love for food.

After they finished their lunch, James clapped his hands together and smiled toward Noelle. "Are you ready to get to work?" he asked.

"Now?" Noelle was trying to quickly brainstorm another idea to postpone the inevitable. Perhaps she needed to make dessert.

"Yeah, I think so."

"Noelle, get it done with. We'll get a dessert later," Libby instructed.

For being the younger sister, Libby sure was bossy. Noelle thought to herself. She couldn't help but grin though, because her sister knew exactly what she was thinking and called her out on it. She thought that was pretty hilarious, actually.

"Okay," Noelle resolved.

"Should you put on your wedding dress?" James asked.

"What? No. Why?" Noelle's anxiety became evident.

"Well, the clue said something about the wedding day," James reminded her.

"I think that's a great idea!" Libby exclaimed. She had a satisfied look of sheer accomplishment on her face.

"No, that's not a good idea," Noelle thought fast. "I had it preserved. It would cost a ton of money to take it out again," Noelle smiled. *Checkmate*, she thought to herself with pride.

"That is a good point," James agreed. "Do you have another dress you could put on?"

"Do I need a dress?" Noelle felt deflated.

"She did say something about the wedding, Noelle," Libby pushed.

Noelle could see the sense of satisfaction in her sister's eyes. The two were like best friends, Noelle wondered why her sister was hanging her out to dry like this.

"I guess I can find something," Noelle retreated toward her room.

She searched through her closet wanting to find something appealing and attractive, but feeling defeated, like everyone was out to get her. She wondered to herself what her mom could have been thinking having James pay so close attention to her looks. It's been three years since they've seen each other. The stress of being a single mom and then having your most supportive person in the world pass away, made the aging process happen in a lot less of a friendly way than it would have if she were to have everything work out the way she had intended. She looked older, more tired.

She thought how James was probably dating some young fresh out of college woman, or perhaps a tiny, pretty and petite Japanese woman; and here she is feeling like an old housewife- without the glory of even carrying the label of wife. She sighed.

"Just get it over with," she reminded herself. She didn't have a choice, this was for other people as well. It didn't just affect her. Had it, she would have likely quit a long time ago. Then she wondered if that thought was true. She would have done anything to feel closer to her mom. She had to admit, this did just that. She was definitely feeling her mom's presence with all these tasks she's had to do as of late. She wasn't ready to admit it, but it did feel kind of nice.

The dress was red. Probably the opposite of weddings, however, it was the only one that Noelle thought would be ideal. She didn't want to throw on a party dress and she sure wasn't putting on anything she would wear to church, so she decided the 50's style red polka dot dress would be just fine. Besides, she couldn't help but think that she was at least a little flattering in it. Not to leave out that it conveniently matched her toenails.

Noelle retraced her eyeliner, just to smoothen the lines up some, and added a coat of mascara. She applied some shiny lip gloss and decided that she was going to have to do, just like that. She didn't know why she bothered with the makeup, he was sculpting her in clay; it wasn't like anyone would see the makeup anyway, but whatever, it made her feel good.

A few minutes later, Noelle casually walked into the kitchen. Her sister gasped, making a scene. This was the exact opposite reaction that Noelle wanted. She hated being the center of attention. She did a lot better behind the scenes. However, Noelle did feel flattered when James noticed.

"Noelle, you look... stunning."

"Thanks," Noelle blushed.

Libby grinned knowing that her reaction and demands were working. She was bound and determined to get Noelle to see that James was still head-over-heels in love with Noelle. She wasn't sure if either of them really realized it yet, but she knew they would sooner or later. She would make sure of that.

"Mom, you look pretty," Levi said as he traced some of the polka dots on his mother's dress.

"Thank you! You are very handsome," Noelle replied.

"So, where do you want me?" Noelle asked. Then she giggled, realizing she sounded far less graceful than she had intended.

James, ignoring the possible connotations, asked her where she would feel most comfortable. He explained to her that she needed to be somewhere around a table, but he didn't mind if she was on a couch or a chair, as long as she felt relaxed and could hold the position for a while without too much movement.

Noelle decided the couch would be the best spot. At least that way she could put her feet up while he did his work. James agreed. He set everything he would need up on the table and told Noelle that she could read a book or watch TV for a bit. He said he was going to work his way from the bottom to the top. He would let her know when he wanted her to smile. Noelle nodded as she felt the shyness overcome her again.

The thought of his eyes staring at her while he sculpted his vision of her on clay was somehow, both, very sexy and nerve-wracking simultaneously. She thought to their first date and how she was so nervous she had thrown on several different outfits just to make sure what she was wearing was perfect. She had told her mom, 'I want him to like me for me, but I want to look good too.' Grace would laugh and tell her that it didn't matter what she was wearing, she was always just as beautiful. Noelle smiled at the memory.

"What's so funny?" James asked.

"Nothing. I was just remembering our first date and how I searched all over for the right thing to wear," Noelle admitted

"I remember. You wore a denim skirt and that bright green sweater," James grinned.

"Yeah. It took me about fifteen outfits to finally decide on that one," Noelle laughed.

"Do you remember when you spilled the water all over the table? Right after the waitress cleaned it up, you spilled another glass. You were so embarrassed!" James was cracking up.

"Oh my gosh, that poor waitress must have thought I was doing it on purpose!" Noelle exclaimed.

"I tipped her good that night," James admitted.

"I couldn't help it, I was so nervous."

"It was cute."

"I was soaked by the time we left. I had even found a seed from one of the lemons in the crease of my skirt."

My plate had some water on it."

"I can't believe you ever asked me out again!"

"How could I not? You were beautiful and so apologetic. It was refreshing dating someone so down to earth and a little clumsy. It made me feel more confident!" James laughed.

Noelle blushed. She remembered that date perfectly. She had realized at that dinner by the way he responded to her, that she was totally in love with him. She just knew they would be married.

"What are you thinking about?" he asked, breaking her concentration.

"I don't know, I was just remembering that date. That was the day I knew we were going to get married."

"Really? After the first date?"

"Yeah. You were such a gentleman about everything. I knew you were a good guy."

"That's funny. I had thought the same that very same date. You were sweet and so humble. I knew then that you would be the perfect wife..." James trailed off. He too, seemed to be lost in thought. Quietly, he got to work on the sculpture.

Noelle allowed her mind to wander off to different parts of their relationship. She remembered the day he proposed and how nervous he was. He was down on one knee, hands shaking, he was trembling so bad that she had to help him put the ring on her finger. Her heart palpitated at the bittersweet memory.

"What happened to us?" she accidentally thought out loud.

"I was just wondering the same. Just one day it ended. Just like that. No warning, nothing. Just crashed down instantly."

"I was lonely," Noelle defended herself.

"I know. I tried so hard to provide you guys with a good life that I forgot to actually live it with you," James admitted.

"I guess that's something to remember with your current girlfriend," Noelle tried to sound innocent when she said it, but she knew there was some level of hurt or disappointment that came out with the words.

"Noelle..."

"Mommy, Aunt Libby had to smell the dirty diaper!" Levi screamed through his laughter. He came running into the room with some kind of card and a rotten smell that trailed after him.

"You won, huh bud?" Noelle forced a smile. She never wanted her son involved in their pain.

"Yup. I won big time! Aunt Libby almost threw up! It was awesome!"

"What kind of game is that?" James asked, his curiosity could no longer be contained.

"It's a smelling game. You have to guess what you're smelling." Levi explained.

"That sounds... intriguing," James rustled his son's hair.

"Levi, let's play another game." Libby came running into the back room where Noelle and James were at. Immediately she sensed the tension and gave Noelle a confused look. Apparently, tension was the last thing she anticipated happening.

Noelle pretended not to notice her sister's inquisitive glance. She just looked at Levi and wished him luck on the next game. Levi ran out of the room as if he were on a major mission. James' smile lightened the tension from the earlier conversation. Quietly, he started kneading the clay. Noelle was lost in her own world as the silence sat comfortably between them.

After a few minutes, James snapped her back to reality. "Do you remember when your mom was walking you down the aisle? You were so nervous, you giggled all the way to the front. People were wondering if you were laughing or crying. Your laughter just filled the room."

"Yeah, I can't believe I did that!" Noelle chuckled at the memory.

"That was the best day of my life," James admitted.

Noelle's eyes welled up at the statement. No matter how hard she tried, she couldn't keep the moisture that was building up, in. She refused to blink. She didn't want him to see her cry. Ever so delicately she tilted her head to the side, just a smidgen, to try and get the tears to run down the opposite cheek, away from his scope of vision. One obstinate tear refused to cooperate. It sneaked out of her eye and found its way down her cheek, dripped down her chin, and puddled up onto her neck. She, carefully, not wanting to make a scene tried to wipe it away. But it was too late. James had already noticed.

He put down the knife he was using to cut and mold the clay and then wiping his hands on a towel, he walked over to the couch where Noelle was laying. Carefully, he sat at the edge of the couch by her waist.

"It's okay," he said as he wiped the tears from her cheeks.

She could feel the roughness of the dried clay on his hands along with his warmth. She closed her eyes, allowing herself to be vulnerable for only a moment. She didn't say anything, but the tears were increasing, and she already knew he knew what she was feeling.

"Shh. I'm right here. You're okay," James said. His eyes were shut too. Peeking at him, Noelle swore that she saw the moisture forming around his eyes. She realized she must have just been imagining it, James never cried. Slowly, he bent down and kissed her on the forehead. "You're okay," he said again, this time in a soft whisper. He stroked her cheek softly, his cheek now resting against her forehead. "Come here," he said as he shifted his weight under hers, fully embracing her.

Her head laying against his chest, she let out the lulling sobs, quietly as possible. She could feel his strength against her. His smell, the same smell she remembered from years ago, enveloping her. Peace and comfort surrounding her. The roughness of his hands against her cheeks. The taste of salt forming in her mouth. All senses engaged, for the first time in years, they were engaged with her husband.

It was then, the first time she was willing to admit it in years, that she was actually, truly in love with James. Sure, she would deny the fact later, she had to in order to save face. However, this moment, right now, she knew that she had made a mistake when she left him. Her mother must have known it too. Wasn't that what this was all about?

James carefully stroked her hair. "I've missed you," he said. The statement that she thought would have made her happy, brought forth anger instead. The raw feeling of that emotion made her brave.

"If you've missed me then why on earth didn't you come for me? Why did you just let me go? You didn't miss me. You were probably having an affair. Just like you're doing now! I'm sure you have some girlfriend, somewhere. I bet she wouldn't like you saying those things to me. Does she even know that our divorce isn't final?" Noelle wouldn't quiet down. Her voice was getting a little bit louder with each sentence.

"Shhh. Noelle, just listen," James started.

"Don't tell me to listen. My heart broke, James. It broke. I was left all alone with a little boy and had to decide what to do. You quit coming home for the holidays, birthdays, everything. You left us alone. You chose work over us- your family. I tried to tell you then. But you didn't listen. That's when I was forced to make a decision. That was the hardest decision of my life. I loved you. With all of me, James, I love you!" Whatever restraint Noelle was holding onto, broke. The sobs were deep, they were heavy. All of her words, all of her feelings over the past three years and for a while longer, poured out of her soul. There was no stopping her.

"I waited for you, James. Every night, I tossed and turned waiting for you to show up. To apologize. To understand and make this work. Every single day I waited. Each night I would go to bed and my heart would break again. Levi, he was so full of questions. He was just a little boy. Don't you see it, James? He loves you. He needs you. Why couldn't you just be honest? Why couldn't you just tell us that there was someone else, or that you just didn't care anymore? Why did you have to just do this to us?" Noelle was pacing the room.

James was sitting on the couch with his head in his hands. "Noelle, just listen."

"No. You listen to me. Did you know when I bought the plane tickets, when I moved us, I bought us both two-way tickets? You didn't know that did you? I *knew* you would come after us. I *knew* you loved us enough that you would apologize. I had no doubt in my mind. Do you realize how small I felt, how surprised I was, that you never even called? I was broken, James. I thought we had so much more than we did. I thought for sure we were something special. I had no idea how wrong I was." Noelle sat on the edge of the couch, breathless. She was scrunched over in her red polka dot dress, holding her stomach. She felt like she was going to throw up, but she also felt relieved at the same time. She didn't realize how long she had been bottling that in.

"Noelle, I'm so, so sorry," James stated quietly.

"Three years later you're sorry? What about then?" Noelle glared at him. Her green eyes three shades darker and two times smaller. She was burning a hole in his soul with that look.

"Can I please explain?" he asked softly.

"Humor me."

"Look, I'm so sorry to interrupt. Noelle, your phone was ringing like crazy. I answered it. I know you're on vacation and everything, but apparently one of your people fell and they had to do an incident report, but you have the key and the other key is lost. They need you to get the key to them right away so they can document what had happened so there is no legal trouble," Libby looked at them nervously. She could feel the tension in the room as soon as she walked in. She was hopeful they would work things out, but it didn't look like that was going to happen.

"Thanks," Noelle said as she wiped the mess off her face. "I need to go. I guess we can finish this sculpture thing later." Just like that she left the room.

James was left sitting on the couch, his head was tilted back, hands clasped together. He looked at Libby and forced a smile.

"Sorry. I didn't mean to interrupt your conversation," Libby stated.

"It's not your fault," James said.

"Just so you know, she's been needing to tell you off for a while now, but she still cares about you."

"I know," James said shaking his head.

"Look, it might be easier if you just tell her the truth. Maybe you guys can just get the divorce finalized. At least for her that would be closure," Libby explained.

James nodded. "What if that's not what I want?" he asked.

"Then you might want to have a really good reason why you never went after her," Libby smiled. "And you should probably want to break up with whoever you're seeing, or she won't give you a second thought."

"I'm not seeing anyone," James admitted.

"She thinks you are. I think she believes you had been this whole time," Libby explained.

"Where does she get that idea from?" he asked.

"Dude, you've been gone for weeks at a time. You were missing out on everything. She was raising a kid by herself. It was apparent that you weren't really prioritizing your family. I'm not trying to be rude, but you asked," Libby stated.

"It wasn't like that. I was so slammed. They had me working this deal to the bone. It was the biggest deal of my life. Do you realize, we just closed with them? Just. Had I known it was going to cost me my whole family, my life, my happiness, don't you think I would have walked away? They kept hinting at closing. One more tweak here, one more situation there. I was missing out on a lot, but I had figured, if I just do what they want me to do, I could walk away when it was done and never have to go back. Granted, I didn't realize that they were going to make us have to change almost everything. I didn't realize that a month would turn to years. If I could go back in time and do things differently, I would. I just wanted to finish this project and then Noelle and Levi would have me forever, because that project would have put me into retirement."

"Why didn't you tell her that?"

"I didn't want to get her hopes up. This project was a multi-billion dollar sale. From that, I could have retired, paid off all my debt, sold the company, and never have to worry about money again. Do you know how bad I wanted that for her? I know that you guys struggled growing up after your dad died. My idea would have paid off all of your debt. Grace's, yours, not to leave out Noelle. She would have been set for life. After I read the letter, I knew she was upset. I decided to let her cool down for a bit while I finished the deal. We were at the finish line. Libby I swear, that's what I had thought. I kept telling myself that, over and over again. The whole time I kept thinking, we're almost done, I will go back and tell them what happened. It ended up we just finished the project the week the lawyer contacted me to come here."

"Seriously?" Libby asked, her doubt evident.

"Look, here, I can prove it." James pulled out his cell phone and showed Libby an email he received from an employee. The date on the email was Dec. 11th. Libby looked at James, surprised.

"You're serious," she stated. "Well why don't you just tell Noelle that?"

"Libby, I've tried. Twice now. But what am I supposed to say? She's so heartbroken and I caused this. I didn't mean to put money ahead of family, I just thought it would smooth over. I wanted the best for her. Do you know how bad I hurt when she left me? To know that it was all my fault, that I could have prevented this. It killed me inside."

"It hurt her too," Libby reminded him.

"I know."

"And Levi."

"I know. My son barely recognized me. What kind of dad does that make me? I wanted so bad for them to be happy, all the while, I didn't realize I was the one taking their happiness away." James put his head in his hands.

Libby reached over and rubbed his back. "Just tell her."

"There was never another woman. You know what your sister means to me. How could I ever replace her?"

"Trust me, it's impossible- I've tried a few times in my life," Libby smiled.

James laughed. Levi walked in crawled into his dad's lap.

"Do you want to play a game now, Dad?" Levi asked.

Wiping the tears from his eyes he said, "Of course I do, son."

Chapter Six
The Sculpture

It didn't take long before Noelle walked back into the home. The red dress flowing behind her, she demanded the attention of everyone in the room.

"Sorry about that," she said. It was apparent she was in a better mood than she was before she left.

"No worries," James said. "Do you want to finish the sculpture now, or should we wait until later?" he asked, cutting to the chase.

"I have an idea," Libby interrupted. "Why don't we order pizza and then me and Levi can do exactly what the note says and watch James do the sculpture as we cheer him on? That was exactly what it said, right?"

Noelle looked at her sister and smiled. "Pizza?" she asked. "Why don't I just make us a pizza?"

"The point is, so you don't have to cook, and we can get this portion of the clue done without further ado, and then tomorrow we'll go find the dentist." Libby thought she was a genius.

"Lib, it's almost Christmas time. Trust me, I'd rather cook than spend $60.00 on pizza," Noelle glanced at her and then nodded toward Levi as if she was telling her telepathically that she still has some Christmas shopping to do.

"Oh, Noelle. It's fine. I'm sure James or I could cover it. No worries, you've been cooking for us this whole time and we don't even know how many more meals you'll have to make. We can do this one," Libby smiled and then glanced at James who nodded.

Noelle bit her bottom lip. "I mean, that's up to you guys."

"Pizza it is. Libs, do you want to call and I'll give you my card? See if they'll deliver it, if not, I don't mind picking it up," James said.

"They'll deliver. I'll use your card. I'll pay the tip since I have cash on me," Libby offered.

James nodded and gave her a thumbs up. Noelle looked at them like they were crazy. She wasn't sure if it was just her or if something was going on. She felt like there was something just a little different in the air. Regardless, she had enough of the emotional stuff and could use the break. Pizza seemed to be the perfect idea.

"Do I still need to wear this dress, or can I take it off?" Noelle asked. She never did appreciate dressing up, not like Libby did. Libby was the type of female to demand attention. Noelle was more of the tomboy type. She was good at sports but hated prom. Noelle had dark hair, Libby had blonde hair. They were almost direct opposites. It was hard to tell they were sisters.

"My vote is to keep the dress on," Libby smiled and nodded toward James.

"I have to say, I agree," James said with a smirk.

Libby could see the passion he had for Noelle all over his face. She wondered why Noelle was so oblivious to it.

"Mom, you look beautiful. Keep it on!" Levi said. "But be careful not to spill pizza on it!" he added.

Everyone laughed. "If anyone were to spill pizza on a dress it would be Noelle," Libby shook her head.

"That's the truth!" Noelle agreed with a smile.

Before long, with far less tension in the air, Noelle was propped up on the couch eating pizza. James had himself a slice and then started etching the clay again. This time, with Libby and Levi watching and cheering him on. Libby had to do everything she could to keep Levi from bumping his dad, but he did a pretty good job after James gave him some clay of his own to play with. Together, James and Levi were both sculpting Noelle.

After about an hour, Noelle could feel James' eyes studying her face. She started to feel a little self-conscious. Her face was turning red as his eyes were fixed on hers. Absentmindedly she closed her eyes and also sucked her teeth, just to make sure there was nothing stuck in them.

"Noey, I need you to open your eyes and smile," James said, quietly. He was deep into his work; intricately shaving off pieces of clay at a time. "So beautiful," he said.

Noelle's face grew hot. Her heart was pounding against her ribcage. She thought it was strange that James was the only person who has ever had that effect on her. Libby started to snicker in the background. Noelle shot her a look. Libby laughed harder. Noelle tried to sneak in an eye roll without James noticing.

"Mom! Stay still. I'm trying to get the perfect picture of your eyes and you keep moving!" Levi was studying her just as hard as James was.

The room erupted into laughter. "Okay, okay, I'm sorry!" Noelle exclaimed.

Libby stuck her tongue out at her sister, happy that Levi called her out for rolling her eyes. Noelle's curiosity was driving her insane. The way James would stare at her with a half of smile on his face, his eyes so tender and warm, the way he would look at his art and gently bite his bottom lip as if her were deep in thought, Noelle wanted so badly to know what was going through his mind. However, she also wanted so badly to let him know that he hurt her, but she wanted him back again, regardless. She scolded her brain for being dumb, thinking like that. Who was she kidding, Noelle was a fool for James.

Moments later, James took a deep breath. He called Libby over to him and asked her to take a peek. "I wish I could catch the essence of her beauty, but it's more in her soul. This feels kind of empty, kind of like a shell of who she is," James said.

"It looks good to me! James, it looks just like her!"

"It's missing what makes her, her."

"You're being too hard on yourself. It's perfect!"

Noelle wanted to get up and see what they were talking about. She started to move, but immediately Libby and James told her, "No, don't move!" Reluctantly, she repositioned herself back on the couch the way she was. Curiosity was burning a hole in her gut.

"Daddy, that looks just like mom!"

James shook his head. "It's missing something. It's driving me insane."

He bore a hole through her heart as he studied her. She reminded herself that he was doing this for a game, that he wouldn't be looking at her like that if it wasn't for the clue. She felt her emotions flatten a little, but she continued to smile as instructed. James grabbed the knife and etched some more of the clay. Libby was just silent standing there with her hand over her mouth in disbelief.

"I can't do anything else with it. I guess this is going to have to do," James said as he placed the knife in a cup of water.

"James, it's perfect!" Libby said studying the sculpture of her sister. "I can't believe how much it looks like her!" She was sincerely impressed.

"It's empty... lacking something... I just wish I could figure out what..."

Noelle could see that he was displeased, with her curiosity boiling over, she couldn't wait any longer to peek at the statue. She gasped. Staring at her was... her. It was perfect. She had no idea James had talent like that. She wondered how her mom knew. Every detail, every shadow, line, curve of her body, every part of her was captured with intricate detail. She was so amazed... so flattered, she could barely swallow.

"James, this is gorgeous!" She was being honest. It was stunning.

James shook his head no. His frustration was very evident. "It's... I don't know... it's just not you."

"How could you say that? It's like my identical twin in a miniature format," Noelle was flabbergasted.

"Sure, it kind of looks like you, but it's missing the most important parts. For instance, your eyes, they are some magnificent color between olive and emerald. The clay is stone colored. It misses the true essence. And the way your eyes shine when you grin, one can see your emotion, even when your face is the same, you can just tell exactly what you're feeling. That's gone from here," he placed his hand against her cheek softly. "Noey, your warmth is visible to even the blindest of men. You are kind, welcoming, but also courageous. Beautiful, but also humble. Sweet and sensitive, but also tough. This is just hollow. Empty. It's not really you enough and it's driving me insane because I can't fix it!"

Noelle could feel her heart beat in her throat. She wanted to keep the feeling that was flooding her body, forever. For a moment, she forgot she was not with him anymore. She forgot that she questioned his love for her or another woman. It didn't matter that he hurt her, that was no longer an issue. For a split moment, she was in a perfect world with she and her husband, holding hands, walking through a field of dandelions with six kids running around them and the sound a stream just barely off in a distance. For a moment she was Mrs. James Miller again.

That moment only lasted a few seconds and then she remembered what it was she was supposed to be doing. The clue. She took a deep breath and then tuned herself in to reality. They were here, present, for one reason and one reason only- to solve her mom's clues. Interrupting the deafening silence between them, she asked, "What's the rest of the clue?" The moment was lost forever.

"This is the clue right here..."

**LOOK AT THIS YOU DID IT AGAIN
I SMILE AS I PICTURE NOELLE'S BIG GRIN
LARGE EYES THAT ARE GREEN AND HAIR SO BROWN
I REMEMBER HER BEAUTY IN HER WEDDING GOWN
JAMES NOW ITS YOUR TURN
REMEMBER THE PASSION THE WAY IT WOULD BURN
WHEN YOU SAW MY DAUGHTER WALKING DOWN THE AISLE
I WANT YOU TO SCULPT HER AND THAT BEAUTIFUL SMILE
TAKE YOUR TIME WITH EVERY DETAIL AND LINE
THE REST OF YOU ENCOURAGE HIM HE'S DOING FINE
WHEN YOU'RE DONE THIS IS WHAT YOU DO
TAKE IT TO THE DENTIST WITH THE FUNNY SHOE
HE'S THE ONE THAT MADE HER SMILE GLINT
ALSO THE ONE WITH YOUR NEXT HINT**

"Who's the dentist with the funny shoe?" James asked.

"I was wondering the same," Libby said. "Noelle, do you remember a dentist with a funny shoe?" she asked.

"I'm not sure. I've had a few dentists, and some were orthodontists. I guess I've had a lot of mouth work done. I'm trying to remember anything unusual about their feet though. I don't recall," she said.

Noelle pondered that one for a moment.

"Well it's too late to go anywhere tonight, anyway. Tomorrow is our last chance for the dentist because after that it will be the weekend. I doubt they're open then," James reminded them.

"James, are you sure you're okay being away from work for so long? Christmas is just over a week away, is this hurting you or any of your holiday plans?" Noelle looked at him for a moment. Part of her felt accusatory, but the other part kind of felt bad for him having to be here for so long, unexpectedly like this.

"No worries. I'm good. I took some time off," James replied.

"What are you doing for Christmas, James?" Libby asked, lightening the mood.

"I guess I'm not sure yet. I could always go visit my parents. I don't know, if you wanted or if it wasn't an intrusion, I could stay here with you guys. It's been a while since I've had a Christmas with Levi."

"Oh, we wouldn't mind at all!" Libby said.

Noelle just about choked. "Don't you have plans already?" she asked.

"Not particularly. I mean, I could make some if this is too much to ask," James replied.

"Not too much at all!" Libby stated.

It was Levi to make the final decision. "Yes! Dad we can open presents! And Mom makes the best cookies ever! You need to try her Rudolph noses, those are my favorite!"

"That's funny. Those are my favorite too!" James said.

The three of them looked at Noelle expectantly. She shrugged. "I guess we have Christmas plans," she said.

Her throat felt like it was closing. She walked over to the fridge and grabbed some water. She could barely believe this was happening. This whole time she's survived, three Christmases without James and now he's going to be spending Christmas with them? And what about afterwards, she's going to have to experience the loneliness all over again. Her heart ached already. Levi, she knew, was going to be distraught. She couldn't possibly tell him that he couldn't stay, she would be the bad guy.

Noelle slipped into her boots and grabbed her coat. "I need some air right quick," she said, smiling. James caught her eye and she could tell that he knew she was concerned. It didn't matter, she realized she may be in tears in a moment and now was a good time to ground herself and think. She quietly closed the door behind her.

James hated to see Noelle like this, but he also knew he was the cause of it. He wanted to rectify this entire situation. It felt so good to him to be with his family again. He had missed them. He couldn't believe it had been three years. He tried to do the right things, but nothing mattered. The company wanted things specific. Every time they thought they had it right, they put different demands on them. He should have left and fixed his marriage. He realized he took them for granted. However, three years passed in no time at all. Things had changed. He couldn't bear to hurt them again, but he couldn't bear the thought of losing them again, either. He decided he would leave Noelle to her thoughts. It never benefited anyone for him to try and get her to talk if she wasn't ready. He knew they were going to have to have a conversation soon, though. He just hoped he was able to say the words he means in a way that she will hear them.

"It's okay, you know," Libby said, interrupting James' thoughts. "She does this sometimes."

"I know. I just wish I could talk to her, but she's not in the mood to hear me out," James replied.

"You'll get your chance. I'm sure of that."

"I just hope when I do, it's not too late."

"It's never too late."

James looked at Libby and smiled. "You're the best sister-in-law a guy could ask for."

"You're not so bad yourself! I just hope that you can stay my brother-in-law!" she laughed.

"Me too," he agreed. James glanced at his son and grinned. He quickly picked Levi up and flew him through the air. "You should get ready for bed, buddy," he said after a few minutes.

"Can you fly me again when I put pajamas on?"

"Why not?" James laughed. The whole time he was watching the door, waiting for Noelle to come back.

Noelle walked down the street deeply taking in the cold air. It stung her lungs but felt good at the same time. She glanced down the street behind her, hoping that James would be following after her, but he wasn't. She wasn't overly surprised. She's come to realize that James wasn't the kind of guy to go chasing her down. She wanted to talk to him, to hear him, but there was really nothing to talk about. She wondered how Christmas would feel having him there with her. She also wondered if she were supposed to get him gifts and then if so, what? These were the moments she missed her mother the most.

"Mom, just tell me what to do. What do I say? Am I being foolish? Why do I love him after all this time? What's wrong with me? Why can't I be strong like you?" The tears spilled down her cheeks and in the cold air, they started to freeze. "Mom, I need you." Noelle closed her eyes and pictured her mother holding her hand, telling her that everything was okay. She smiled as she thought about the clues. She knew her mom spent her last days coming up with this little game for them and she cherished it. She was grateful. She just wished she could control her emotions better.

"Mom, please show me a sign that says I'm going to be okay. Please show me that you're with me." Noelle walked on, remembering how she had been on this same stretch of road when she learned how to ride her bike. She remembered screaming and crying and being so upset when her mother let her go and she fell. *"You promised you wouldn't leave me!"* She had cried.

Grace laughed. "You're okay. I'm right here. I will never leave you. I promise."

"You're gone now, Mom. I'm not ready to face everything alone. I still need you." The tears were streaming down her cheeks. Noelle had never felt so alone.

The wind picked up and Noelle bundled her coat around her tighter. Wiping her face off, she turned around to start heading for home. Her fingers and toes were starting to go numb. Her ears were burning they were so cold. She had guessed that it was only about 15 degrees outside. The wind picked up again and that is when Noelle saw it. A perfectly white feather started to bounce off the snow filled street and make its way toward her.

Chasing after it, Noelle giggled. There was never a pure white feather in the middle of December, in the freezing cold weather of Michigan. She knew beyond a shadow of a doubt that it was her mother telling her that she was going to be okay. Grabbing the feather, Noelle immediately felt refreshed. She knew no matter what happened, she could face it and she wouldn't be alone. With a renewed sense of hope, she thanked her mother and then continued her way toward home.

Walking up the driveway, Noelle paused a moment as she approached the house. She could see James, with a carefree smile on his face, flying their son through the air like an airplane or perhaps in Levi's mind, a superhero. She stood outside of the picture window watching them. Everyone was laughing. Libby with her beautiful blonde curls falling down her back, James so strong and tender, and Levi carefree and full of love, Noelle felt the warmth overcome her. It didn't matter what the future held, she knew that at this moment all was as it was meant to be.

Taking a deep breath, prepared to face the ups and downs of her emotions, Noelle walked into her home. Her smile was warm and sincere and when she and James connected eyes, she saw a sense of peace wash over him. Regardless of her future, Noelle, was with her family this Christmas thanks to her mother, and she felt true gratitude for it. She didn't have to be alone.

Noelle, still holding the feather, set her coat on the chair and then carefully, put the feather in a vase near her bed. She was shivering as she walked out of the room toward her family.

"Noelle, you're freezing," James said. "Come here," he said as he patted the spot on the loveseat next to him and handed her the throw that was sitting there.

Noelle plopped down and happily grabbed the blanket.

"Oh man, your hands are like ice. Here," James grabbed her hands and brought them to his mouth and blew on them. Her whole entire body broke out in goosebumps. He rubbed her fingers between his palms, producing not only heat but in Noelle's case, raw emotion. Not really knowing if it was intentional or if her body was trying to warm itself, Noelle started to shiver.

James grabbed the throw and pulled it up over Noelle. Then he wrapped his arms around her really tight. He pulled her close to him and placed his cheek gently against one of her ears for a few moments and then did the same with the other one.

Noelle's body was physically cold, but she felt as if she were emerging sparks. The heat traveled down her spine and the surplus of energy went straight to her heart and her head. Her heart was racing as James encapsulated her. Her head was spinning, she felt as if she were a teenage girl with her first crush.

Noelle brought her knees to her chin and that's when James leaned into her and grabbed her toes. He then wrapped his arms around her and brought his feet up against hers, warming them too. "You're like ice." He took his socks off and pulled them onto Noelle's feet.

Libby laughed. "That's a way to warm a woman up, James. Put your dirty socks on her." They erupted in laughter.

"Well, they are warm," he said, shrugging.

Noelle started to warm up, but she would never admit it. Sitting there at that moment she was probably the warmest she's ever been in her whole life.

"Mom, will you tuck me in?" Levi rubbed his eyes.

She didn't want to move from her present state of bliss. Taking a deep breath, she started to get up. She was pretty sure she felt James hesitate before letting her go. Instinctively she glanced at her sister, whom she felt typically reads her mind. When Libby cracked a smile, Noelle couldn't help but grin with her feelings of reassurance. Libby rolled her eyes.

Noelle asked Levi if he wanted to sleep in the living room or if he wanted to sleep in his bedroom. He said he wanted to lay in the bed, but he may get up and sleep on the floor later. Noelle smiled, she knew he must be tired if he was willing to go straight to bed. She thought about it and realized between the snowmen, the pizza, the sculptures and everything, he's had a really long day. They all had actually.

She carefully tucked him in and said his prayers with him. Then he gave her a hug and snuggled up to his stuffed dog.

Opening his eyes just a little, he asked her to get his dad so he could say goodnight to him too. Noelle, with tightness in her chest, obliged. Moments later she was witnessing a boy and his father sharing the love and intimacy that only a boy and his father could share. It's a combination of tough and tender. With rustled hair, a punch on the shoulder, a couple of smelly jokes, and a kiss on the forehead, they were two peas in a pod.

On the way back toward the living room, James stopped Noelle in the hallway. Grabbing her hand, he pulled her close to him. He looked her in the eyes and before either realized what was going to happen next, they found themselves engaged in the most passionate kiss they've ever experienced. James and Noelle, Levi's mother and father, after three years of separation, together again. Neither of them was sure what the other was going to do, both of them taking a chance at love, regardless of the consequences.

"I've missed you so much, Noelle," James said. His hand burning a hole in the side of her face. His fingers intertwined in her hair.

"I've missed you too. But there are so many unanswered questions. Right now, this way, it's not going to work. It didn't before. How could this possibly change? What's different, James?" Noelle, her lip trembling, wanted so badly to hear the words, the promises, the apologies. But she wanted them to be true.

"How about this... How about you and I after Christmas is over, sit down and have a talk? We won't worry about it now, we will just have fun finishing these clues for your family and then after that, when the holiday is over, we can schedule a time; just me and you, and we can get it all out? Does that sound okay?" James was pleading with her. His eyes pressing hers, reading her, begging for some form of confirmation.

Noelle nodded. "I think that's a good idea," she agreed.

James smiled. He placed both of his hands on her cheeks and then kissing her one last time, he thanked her. He took a deep breath and gently placed his forehead against hers, "just for the record, I've never stopped loving you," he said.

Noelle allowed the tears to fall down her cheeks. She closed her eyes and melted in his arms. Waiting for after Christmas or not, she couldn't help but relish in the fact that he was there with her now. Her emotions were back and forth on whether or not she was totally in love with him or still bitter over what had happened with their marriage. Regardless of what she was feeling, his arms wrapped around her, holding her, was a place she never wanted to leave again.

Chapter Seven
The Dentist and Sledding

Noelle barely slept a wink that night. She was in the living room five feet from her sister and five feet from James, tossing and turning, her head going through a myriad of images. Would she and James get back together? What was she doing? Could she handle him working in Tokyo again? What about Levi's school, should she change him? Would he even want to be with her again? What about another woman... Was there one? She thought of everything. She hated not having answers. She knew James was right though, it was better to wait after the holidays and discuss it than trying to figure it out in the middle of everything else. So, wait she would.

She got up that morning and put together a quiche. It didn't take long before everyone woke to the aroma of that and the cinnamon rolls she decided to whip together. Soon, they were all surrounding the table, enjoying their breakfast. Noelle smiled. She felt good watching everybody eat her food so intently.

James broke the silence. "Tell me, Levi. What are you asking Santa for?"

Noelle's ears perked up, she still had to do some of her Christmas shopping. She made a mental note to get that done in between all the clue festivities.

"I want a new bike! One without training wheels!" Levi was excited.

"How are you going to ride it in all the snow?" James asked.

"Dad, I'll wait for the snow to go away. Then I will ride it all day every day!"

"Sounds like you have things all planned out!"

"Dad, are you going to be here in the spring time, to watch me ride my bike?" Levi asked as he shoved a big bite of quiche into his mouth.

"We'll see what happens, Buddy," James said, though he was looking at Noelle.

"Let's just take it one day at a time," Noelle cut in.

Libby smiled. "Noelle, if you were to have one thing for Christmas, what would it be?" Libby asked.

"Hmm. That's a tough one…"

"Say money was no object?" Libby added.

"So, I'm rich and can have anything I want?" Noelle asked.

"Yes, but it can't be dumb, no world peace, a healthy family, or anything like that. Something tangible. What would you pick?"

"You mean something material? Hmm. I don't know…"

"Yeah and nothing practical. It can't be like free gas or anything."

"You're giving me a ton of limitations," Noelle said.

"Trust me, I know you, but I'm curious."

"I guess if I could have anything in the whole world and money was no object, I would want a cute, quaint, little restaurant. A family place, full of love, good home-cooking, and wonderful smells. A place people could go to and feel good, like a family." Noelle was holding her fork and smiling. "What would you pick, Libby?"

"A mustang. That's all I want. Nothing more, nothing less. Piece of cake, easy," Libby laughed.

"I knew you would say something like that!"

"I have everything else I could ever want, everything but a mustang that is," Libby laughed and shrugged her shoulders. It was true.

Turning the attention to James, Libby asked him next. "What would you want if you could have anything?"

"I guess I would want a house on Lake Michigan. It would have to have lots of rooms so we could have company and family over. I would like for there to be a firepit and a gazebo. I want a pontoon boat to enjoy a relaxing evening on the lake. I would love a big fireplace with a huge kitchen that Noelle could cook every meal she wanted in. I would love a nice little art studio in the basement. A hammock outside that is big enough to fit two. Several bathrooms all with the jacuzzi tub. I would like a tower so our daughters can pretend to be Rapunzel..." James trailed off with a smile.

"Wow, you thought about this before, haven't you?" Libby asked with a laugh.

"Yeah. Only a time or two," James grinned.

"Could I have a huge playroom?" Levi asked.

"Absolutely! A great big giant one full of toys! And we would have a big driveway, so when Aunt Libby would come over she would have a place to park her shiny new car!"

Levi clapped his hands.

Noelle's heart couldn't take it anymore. She was done when he said something about her in the kitchen. She wondered to herself if that was really what he would want if he had all the money in the world. Quietly, she stood up from the table and placed her plate in the sink. She announced that she was going to take a shower. The conversation at the table continued on as she made her way to the bathroom.

When Noelle finished up, she felt refreshed. She came to the conclusion that she could enjoy the moment she was in and then she and James would figure themselves out soon enough. She tried to recall anything about a dentist with a funny shoe. She had nothing. She towel-dried her hair and threw some clothes on, leaving the bathroom, she was surprised to see that James had left. That was rare. James never went anywhere without taking a shower first.

"Where'd he go?" Noelle asked.

"I don't know. He said he had to hurry up and leave for a minute but that he'd be back by the time everyone was dressed and ready to go," Libby replied.

"Oh."

"Noelle, you know he loves you, right?"

"No, I guess I don't know," Noelle wasn't sure if she was being honest or not. She kind of had a feeling.

"He told me he does. Oh and by the way, there's no other woman."

"How do you know?"

"He told me."

"Yeah, but..."

"But nothing. He's made some mistakes, but you really need to talk to him."

"I will. We're talking after Christmas."

"Good. Then stop being so moody," Libby stated.

"Moody? I haven't been moody!"

"Trust me, you have."

Noelle was taken aback. She didn't think she was being too moody, but if she were being honest with herself she knew she was struggling with all these emotions. At this point, she was almost giddy. Did James actually say to Libby that he loved her? Was he really single? She almost felt giggly. Libby, practically reading her mind, rolled her eyes. Noelle shrugged.

"I have no idea who this dentist is," Noelle changed the subject.

"Neither do I. But I guess we could start with every dentist you remember seeing when you were growing up," Libby suggested.

Noelle nodded. "I can think of four of them, but there may have been more."

"Well, we'll start with those four. Today's Friday, there's no dentist that's going to be in his office on a Saturday or Sunday. Next week's Christmas and I have no idea how many more clues we have to solve. I'd like to get these figured out before Christmas, because I don't want to have to wait until next year to finish," Libby said, remembering the rules.

Noelle nodded her head. She agreed. "I have Christmas shopping and things like that to do too," Noelle reminded her.

"Maybe I'll keep Levi, or me and James can keep Levi, and you can get your shopping done. I have a hunch James may want to go with you, so if he does, that's fine, I'll keep Levi myself. That way you will be able to do what you need to do. Maybe the next day, when we decide to stop with the clues, you three can sit together while I go shopping. I doubt mom would care as long as she knew we were working together. She understood that we have things we have to get done, right?" Libby looked at Noelle expectantly.

"I think she would have realized that. This sounds like a good plan," Noelle agreed.

"Let's write these dentists down, so we have a plan for as soon as James comes back."

It only took James about a half an hour before he came back into the house. Levi was just finishing getting ready.

"Do you need to shower first?" Noelle asked.

"I showered early this morning when everyone was sleeping," James replied.

Noelle must have gotten more sleep than she realized. She didn't know anyone was up before she was.

"Are you guys ready to go finding the next clue?" James asked.

Noelle thought to herself that he appeared to be genuinely happy. Eager even. Regardless, his attitude was contagious because everyone in the car that morning seemed to have a good sense of joy and were looking forward to solving the clues.

"So, we're looking for a dentist with a funny shoe, correct?" James asked.

"Yeah, here's the clue again:"

LOOK AT THIS YOU DID IT AGAIN
I SMILE AS I PICTURE NOELLE'S BIG GRIN
LARGE EYES THAT ARE GREEN AND HAIR SO BROWN
I REMEMBER HER BEAUTY IN HER WEDDING GOWN
JAMES NOW ITS YOUR TURN
REMEMBER THE PASSION THE WAY IT WOULD BURN
WHEN YOU SAW MY DAUGHTER WALKING DOWN THE AISLE
I WANT YOU TO SCULPT HER AND THAT BEAUTIFUL SMILE
TAKE YOUR TIME WITH EVERY DETAIL AND LINE
THE REST OF YOU ENCOURAGE HIM HE'S DOING FINE

WHEN YOU'RE DONE THIS IS WHAT YOU DO
TAKE IT TO THE DENTIST WITH THE FUNNY SHOE
HE'S THE ONE THAT MADE HER SMILE GLINT
ALSO THE ONE WITH YOUR NEXT HINT

"Noelle, you don't remember anything regarding a dentist and a funny shoe?" James asked.

"No. I've wracked my brain over that for the past couple of days. I got nothing."

"Well, I think we can start with the list of dentists you've seen in the past. That may help. James did you remember the sculpture?" Libby asked.

"Yes, I have it."

"I feel kind of silly about giving a random dentist a sculpture of me," Noelle stated candidly.

"Honestly, Noelle, I don't blame you. I would feel silly too," Libby nodded in agreement.

"Don't tell him it's you, maybe he will never figure it out," James offered.

"It looks just like Mom," Levi said. Nobody could really argue that point, knowing that Levi was right. No matter if they stated it or not, the statue really looked a lot like Noelle.

They drove to the closest dentist's office on the list first. Much simpler than the rest of their tasks, sitting outside in the middle of the yard was a huge statue of a shoe with a giant smile.

"That's a funny shoe!" Levi said, laughing.

"There's no way this is it, that was way too easy!" Libby said, laughing.

"There's only one way to find out," James grabbed the statue as he opened the door to the car.

"What are you going to do, just hand it to him and ask for the clue?" Noelle felt perplexed.

"Sure, why not? That's the only way we'll ever know." James shrugged.

Walking away with the statue in tote, James opened the door to the dentist office. Noelle looked at Libby as if she were wondering if they should follow. Libby shrugged her shoulders. Together the three followed suit. By the time they got to the door, James was already in there talking to the dentist.

"Noelle, your smile is looking wonderful. Seems I did a good job!" The dentist stated.

As soon as she heard him speak, she remembered. He was a sculptor by hobby. He loved art. He would say that is what kept him sane. "Thank you!" Noelle said, smiling.

"Your mother told me that your husband was a wonderful artist! She asked me for a favor, so I asked for one in return. I asked her to have your husband sculpt something he was passionate about. He does a great job, it looks exactly like you!"

"Thank you."

"Even more, it's nice to see that you're his passion!"

"Well, that's kind of a funny story-" Noelle started.

"-She is my biggest passion," James interrupted.

The dentist grinned and nodded. "I can tell. The intricate detail on this statue. Tell me, James, do you ever consider sculpting ice?" The dentist asked.

James could tell there was a purpose to his question.

"I guess I don't know." James answered honestly.

"Well, if you try it and if you're interested, I would love to have you do some ice sculptures for me."

James nodded. "If so, I will let you know," James agreed thoughtfully. "Before we go, do you happen to have a clue that Grace would have left for us?"

"A clue? Not that I know of... No, not that I recall."

"Are you sure? My mom said that if we gave you the sculpture, you would give us the clue we are looking for," Libby explained.

"Nope, can't say that I have a clue of any type," the dentist looked a little confused.

"Did Grace leave anything for us for when we came for the sculpture?" James asked.

"Hmm, not that I know of. I was supposed to give you the receipt, but that's the only thing I can think of," he said. "I'm sorry I couldn't be of further assistance."

"No, that's okay... Do you happen to have the receipt for us?" James asked thoughtfully.

"Yup, it's right here." He handed them a folded receipt paper.

James took it and smiled. "Thank you so much for the offer, I will contact you about the ice sculptor," James shook the dentist's hand.

"I look forward to it. Have a Merry Christmas!"

"Merry Christmas to you too," The four replied.

After heading out the door of the dentist office, Libby was the first to ask if the receipt paper was the clue. James nodded. Opening it up, the look on his face while reading it was priceless. He started to laugh and then handed the clue to the girls. It read:

LIBBY YOU'RE NEXT MY DEAR GIRL
BEAUTIFUL BLONDE HAIR WITH THE GORGEOUS CURL
TO THE CHRISTMAS BALL YOU THREE WILL GO
EACH OF YOU DAZZLED UP WHITE AS THE SNOW
MISTELTOE IS MY FAVORITE PLANT
LIBBY STAND UNDER EACH ONE DON'T TELL ME YOU CAN'T
HOWEVER MANY THERE ARE TWO OR EVEN THREE
UNDER EACH ONE YOU WILL WAIT TO SEE
WHO GOES AHEAD AND KISSES YOU
ITS IN ONE OF THESE LEAVES YOU'LL GET YOUR NEXT CLUE
BY THE WAY THE NIGHT IS YOUNG
NOELLE DON'T BE A DRAG AND GO HAVE SOME FUN
JAMES AND YOU UNDER THE MISTLETOE
DON'T AVOID IT OR THIS I WOULD KNOW

LEVI HAS A SITTER OF THIS I AM SURE SHE IS THE LADY THAT LIVES NEXT DOOR

"Mom must have lost her mind!" Libby sounded panicked.

"She seemed pretty sane to me," Noelle retorted. She had a smile on her face and regardless of if it was nice to do so or not, she was happy Libby was finally getting a little humiliation. Noelle felt that she sure had enough of it, it was about time Libby got a taste of what she's been going through.

James walked to the car with a smirk on his face. By his look, it would appear that he agreed with Noelle, but there was no way he was ever going to admit to it in front of Libby. He didn't want to irritate her more than what she was already irritated. He had to room with her for the next few nights, might as well keep it a peaceful stay. Besides, he could see it being a little creepy having to go to a ball and stand under a mistletoe to see who kisses her. That didn't feel like the safest thing in the world. Not only that, but then having to dig through the plants to find the next clue. As dangerous as that could be for a person- not knowing who would want to steal a kiss, it was funny just the same.

"I can't believe she wants me, her youngest child, to stand under a plant and wait for some random guy to kiss me. This isn't the 60's, didn't she realize that there are crazy people out these days?" Libby whined.

"You'll be fine, Libs. Trust me. There is no way me and James wouldn't be around watching. I wouldn't leave you by yourself if you wanted me to. I would be too curious to see who you're stuck smooching on!" Noelle was cracking up.

Libby folded her arms over her chest and scowled. She was obviously irritated. Her irritation didn't matter to Noelle at all. She knew James would protect her sister. She also knew that there was no way she was ever going to let Libby live this one down.

"When is the ball?" Libby asked, hopeful they missed it.

"That sign right there says it's tomorrow night." James pointed out.

Noelle could tell that he was enjoying this clue as well. She was definitely glad it wasn't her to have to stand under every mistletoe. More so, she found herself secretly excited that the expectation was for her and James to stand under one together as well. To her, this was the best clue yet!

"Well we can't solve this clue until tomorrow. What do you guys want to do in the meanwhile?" James asked.

Noelle couldn't help but think he had something in mind. "I don't know, what were you thinking?"

"Sledding," James said as he smiled.

Noelle looked at Libby. "You game?"

"Anything to take my mind off this dumb dance tomorrow."

"Levi?"

"How could I ever say no to sledding?" He had a giant grin on his face.

"Let's go!"

They stopped at the house to pick up their sleds and in no time at all they were on the hills near Lake Michigan's dunes. It was cold, but it wasn't dangerously cold. Levi and James each grabbed a circular sled to start. James warned Levi how fast it would be. Levi thought the faster the better. The girls followed, wanting to ride together on a long sled.

Levi ran up the hill and in no time at all, Noelle could see him in his bright green coat shooting down the hill, full of laughter. His sled spinned a little, but he seemed to have decent control over it. James followed Levi. He sat on his disc and shot straight down the hill. He leaned into the sled to steer some. Purposefully hitting a bump, James went sailing into the air. Besides a small thud when he came down, he was full of laughter too.

Libby and Noelle were next. Together they sat on their sled. They started down the hill slowly, and then not picking up momentum, they tried to push their way down with their arms. They got stuck in the middle half of the hill. Noelle, bending to push the sled some more, tumbled out of the sled and rolled down the hill. It was Libby who was laughing hysterically. She slowly slid the rest of the way down.

By the time Noelle rolled down the hill, she had to be careful because Levi was already halfway down in his disc again. He didn't know how to steer, so James was yelling at her to look out so he didn't hit her. She quickly got up and moved out of the way as Levi came barreling toward her.

She grabbed a simple, cheap, plastic, green sled. She decided to lay on her belly and go down the hill this time. Once she climbed all the way up, she shimmied her way onto the sled and then hit a small patch of ice. Noelle shot down the hill superfast. She was holding on for dear life. By the time the hill was over, Noelle was still sledding. She slid all the way down the hill and clear across the park. She saw a dog or a deer, she wasn't sure which, leap out of the way as she flew past it. She heard someone screaming, but she wasn't sure if that was her or someone else. By the time the sled was all the way across the park and halfway into the field, it finally slowed down. That was when Noelle decided she was done sledding.

She sat up, dizzy and a little disoriented. She took a deep breath and then checked each part of her body to make sure she wasn't broken. She turned around to see Levi running toward her. James and Libby were shadowing him, though those two were cracking up. Levi had a huge grin on his face when he reached his mother.

"Mom, that was awesome! Can you do it again?" He was excited.

"Not right now, buddy," Noelle said. She wanted to tell him never will she ever slide down a hill again, but she knew that after her nerves calmed down, she would be up there terrorizing herself for fun. Realizing she was not broken, Noelle stood up and pulled the sled along behind her.

"Can I try that sled, Mom?" Levi asked excitedly.

Noelle handed him the sled. "You be careful!"

It was too late, he had already taken off halfway across the park and ready to climb the hill. Noelle laughed, remembering herself at that age.

"That was classy," Libby laughed.

Noelle nodded and smiled, pretending that the experience was intentional.

"Why don't you and I go down together before you totally cash in?" James asked, knowing all to well that Noelle was going to stop for the day. Regardless on how much she would pretend otherwise.

"I don't know. I think I've had enough for one night," She objected.

"Come on, just one time with me. Please?" The hope in his voice is what made Noelle change her mind.

"I suppose we can go down once," Noelle agreed.

Once they got up the hill, James told Noelle he would hold the sled and then he would hop on behind her. She was sitting in the front and then as soon as he got in, he was holding the sled still with his boot.

"Ready?" he asked, wrapping his arms around her.

"Ready."

He hoisted his foot through the snow and kicked off their decline. In no time at all they were sailing down the hill. Together they were laughing as they made their way down. Libby was at the bottom snapping pictures of both of them, she was eager to share them on social media later.

Noelle felt warm and cozy snuggled up to James on the sled. The two were enmeshed together, his hot breath against the back of her neck made her shiver with joy. His laughter, the sound of his voice in her ear felt surreal. Three years was a long time not to be with the one you love. Yet, three years also seemed like yesterday when the one you love was sitting behind you and holding you close, regardless if you're on a snow-covered hill or not. This she was grateful for.

When the sled slowed to a stop, Noelle and James sat there, neither wanting to move, but neither really knowing what else to do. It was Noelle who decided to get up first. She took a deep breath and then slowly worked her way out of the sled. She didn't object when he held her hand as support so she could get up. It didn't matter that she was wearing gloves, she could still feel the heat from his touch sending electric currents through her body.

Libby was still snapping pictures. Levi dove into one of the pictures for an action-packed photobomb. He looked as if he were flying through the air in the photograph. By the time they were ready to head back to the house for dinner, Levi looked like a live, stop-animation snowman. Shuffling like a penguin, with rosy cheeks, Levi declared this day to be the best of his life. Noelle was overjoyed that a Christmas she dreaded so much, was coming out to be so wonderful. Silently she thanked her beloved mother who knew how to make everything okay.

By the time they got home, everyone was ready to eat. Noelle took this upon herself to find something in the kitchen to 'whip up'. When normal people would find something to throw together, it would typically look like a small casserole of some sort, or perhaps a salad or a sandwich. This didn't happen with Noelle. Even when cupboards appeared bare, Noelle could make things appetizing and splendid. She was amazing in the kitchen.

Noelle never pursued cooking as a career. There were a few reasons for this. The first being, she hadn't found her passion before she was married. Noelle, at the time, knew she was a creative person, but she didn't really know what she loved so much she could never get sick of it. At the time, she loved to cook, sew, paint, craft, garden, watch kids, and play a ton of sports. She had always wanted to be a mother and had decided at a young age that she was going to have a big family if all worked out for her. If it didn't, she wanted to be a foster mother. When she started dating James she was working as a waitress in a local diner. She wasn't able to keep that job for very long because she was often disgusted by the food she would be forced to serve people.

It didn't take long for Noelle and James to fall in love. James was finishing his degree and Noelle was going to school part time. Noelle would watch Libby when Grace would have to work nights. Grace was a registered nurse. Money wasn't something Noelle was never too worried about. If she wanted something, she had her part time job, or she would pick up extra kids when Grace left her with Libby and make a few dollars that way. James landed a great job right out of college and then soon after, he proposed to Noelle. It wasn't long after that she moved across the country and then later had Levi.

After Levi was born, Noelle stayed home full time to raise him. She was happy as a clam holding down the fort and spending time with her boy. James made enough money for them to live off of. However, as time went on, James was gone more frequently and Noelle became lonely. That's when she left him.

After heading back to her mother's house, Noelle was able to pick up a job at the school as a teacher's aid. She enjoyed working with the kids, but she felt like something was missing. She found her favorite time of the day was when she was spending it cooking dinner with Levi. Pretty soon, to help the school out, Noelle would put on bake sales and dinner fundraisers to provide more money for art supplies and other things that the school needed.

It didn't take long for people to start putting in requests for Noelle's baked goods and dinners. Pretty soon, she was getting orders every week for different children's birthday cakes and things like that. In order to keep up, Noelle had to quit the job working at the school and focused solely on meeting those requests. Her cakes were a community favorite among birthday parties, anniversary's etc. She has even catered her share of weddings, because her dinners were just as good as her desserts.

Between her work catering and baking and then the money her mom left her from her life insurance, Noelle didn't need for much of anything. She put her mom's life insurance money in savings and hasn't really needed to touch it. James sent a good check to her every month and called that his child support. She never had to argue with him about it, he was more than generous. Overall, she had everything she could ever want.

Noelle loved the idea of opening a small restaurant, but she didn't think it was a smart idea to pursue that, because she would need some loans and she refused to use her house as collateral. She lived in the house her father built her mother. It was all paid off and to be honest, though somewhat small, the house was beautiful. Her mother designed it and her father built it for her. She couldn't bear the thought of things not working out and her losing the house.

    Before Grace had passed, she sat the girls down and discussed financial matters. Grace explained why Noelle was getting the house and Libby was content with that. Noelle liked the house and had a child. Besides, she was already living there. On the flip side, Libby received more money than Noelle did off the life insurance. The reason why was because Noelle got the house. Grace wanted to make sure everything was split as fairly as possible. Both girls agreed and there were never any kinds of arguments regarding the will or any life matters at that. Honestly, Noelle and Libby were more like best friends than sisters.

    Libby, Noelle's direct opposite in every sense of the word, was the flashier sister. In fact, when James and Noelle started to date, people around town were making comments about how James belonged with Libby, not Noelle. Libby was gorgeous, outgoing, talented, and enjoyed the limelight. Noelle was beautiful, but in the more subtle sense. James, like a model himself, put most of the guys in town to shame. He was exquisite. Women adored him. Ironically, once people were to get to know both, Libby and James, neither of them acted like one would expect based off their appearance. Libby was modest, sweet, and very empathetic. She cared about public matters and life. James was kind, gentle, and very smart. He never reacted without assessing the outcomes of each possible reaction.

    Libby graduated from Michigan State University with a nursing degree, very much like her mother. She worked part time and would book gigs singing for events on the weekends. She mostly sang for people at her church, a lot of weddings and funerals and things like that. Her voice was radiant. Often times, Libby and Noelle would be at the same wedding or funeral together; Libby singing, Noelle cooking. Libby bought a giant house full of bedrooms and bathrooms, but never had anyone to share it with. She hardly dated. One reason was because she didn't care too much about relationships. Libby was content with her life. Another reason was because she didn't prioritize the time to pay attention to anyone. She was ambitious and a lot of guys were intimidated by that and she felt she didn't have the time to waste explaining herself.

Noelle served everyone pork chops, baked potatoes, and green beans. Libby looked at her as if she had bigfoot standing behind her ready to pounce on her. "What?" Noelle asked.

Libby shook her head. "I don't know how you get the energy to just do this. Seriously, Noelle, how do you have time to snap the beans, baked the pork chops, and the potatoes, shred the cheese, and everything else, after a full day of sledding? It makes no sense," she said.

"It didn't take much. I just grabbed some things and threw it together. No big deal."

"No, Noelle, tacos you throw together. Salad you throw together. Restaurant food, you don't just throw together. Look at the presentation, how it's seasoned, however every bean is almost the same size. The meat looks delicious and the potato looks like something that came out of a magazine. Perfectly stuffed with cheese that I'm sure you grated yourself. You are a prodigy, Noelle. People pay a lot of money for meals like this and I'm sure it tastes better than the ones people pay for!"

"It does," James agreed, putting a piece of pork chop into his mouth.

Noelle laughed. "Well thank you."

"Noelle, you've waited long enough. Why in the world won't you open your own place? You're more talented than anyone I've ever met." Libby took a bite. "You used fresh sage and basil, didn't you?"

"I grew them myself."

"You would!" Libby laughed, taking another bite.

"If I ever were to open a place, I would require fresh herbs and spices. That's where you get the most robust flavors," Noelle explained.

"Noelle, I would pay you every day to cook for me," Libby said.

"I forgot how good her food was!" James agreed.

"Well thanks everyone, but it is just a hobby. One day I may get a business, but for now, I'm okay with where I'm at," Noelle stared off into space. She thought that she really could make a great restaurant owner. For now, she couldn't even consider such a thing. A single mom, she hadn't the time or the money to consider that option. Not now, anyway.

Once everyone finished up, Noelle had asked Libby if she would mind watching Levi so she could get some shopping done. Libby readily agreed. James overheard the conversation and asked Noelle if she cared if he tagged along. Noelle shrugged, the company may be nice she thought. Her heart knew that it had nothing to do with company, but everything to do with James.

The headed to the local mall. Noelle had some ideas on what to get for her son, though she wasn't really sold on anything yet.

"What about a bike?" James asked.

"Yeah, I thought about that, but that would take up a lot of the budget I planned on for him," Noelle answered truthfully.

"You know that if you ever need money, I'm here," James stated.

"Actually, James, that's where our problems began. You weren't here," Noelle didn't mean to sound rude, but his words stung and she wanted to make sure he sees the reality of what she was dealing with. There was no way she would ask him for financial support. He already paid a ton in child support and he technically didn't have to. They weren't really divorced. James chose to pay for him.

"Ouch," James said. "Noelle, look. I'm here now."

"James, I see you, but you're leaving soon. I can't depend on you being here now. I can't fathom asking you to buy our son a bike when I know I have a budget that I must stick to. I can't worry about when you're around or not. I have to provide for him the best way I know how. If I go all elaborate on him now, then what happens next year? He will be disappointed because I didn't do the same."

"How do you know I won't be around then?" James asked, softly.

"How do I know you will?" Noelle replied. "Look, James, if you want to get him a bike, please be my guest. He would love you for it. But the bike has to come from you, not Santa, and not me. So when next year comes, he will know what he can expect from me and/or Santa and then he won't be upset that this year was so much different."

James looked hurt. Noelle felt bad, but she had no choice but to be honest. Those were the types of decisions she was forced to make as a single mother. "I'm sorry, Noelle. I had no idea..."

"It's fine. But that's why this is hard. I can't depend on much. Sure, there's money in the bank, but I need that in case something happens. This whole time I was worried that if you took me off your health plan, that I would have to have the money to pay for health insurance. Say you're dating someone and decide to get married. I can't continue to be on your health insurance plan. I sure can't afford to go without. I'm a single mom. I have to stay healthy to take care of my son. Nobody else is going to do it."

James cringed at the words, 'single mom.' "Noelle, I wouldn't leave you high and dry like that."

"James, I know you wouldn't mean to. You're a good guy. But maybe your wife would. Stuff happens. People change when they're in love. I know I wouldn't want my future husband paying for his ex-wife's health plan. I need to keep money in the bank for those types of reasons. Make sense?"

James nodded.

"That's why I have to stick to a budget. If I got into the habit of buying everything I wanted to get for Levi, just because it would brighten his day, I wouldn't have any type of safety net. That's not smart. So as boring as it is, a budget is the right thing."

"You're a good mom, Noelle."

That statement stung. She didn't know why, it was a compliment, but it felt final and it stung. She didn't want to just be a 'good mom'. She wanted reassurance, love, companionship, commitment. But that's not what he said. He said she was a 'good mom'.

"Thanks," she replied.

"Well, let's get shopping," James suggested, changing the subject.

Quietly and with a much different feeling in the air, Noelle and James walked through the mall trying to decide on gifts for their son. James didn't mention anything else about the bike, but when they walked past them, Noelle noticed James scoping them out. She didn't say anything about it. She assumed he would probably show up with a bike in hand on Christmas day and to be honest, that would be okay with her, because even though he would be the hero, she knew her son would be ecstatic.

After a few eerily quiet hours, Noelle had picked out some Christmas gifts for her son. Because she couldn't afford a bike, she had settled for a scooter that costed approximately $50.00 less than the bikes did. Adding a few coupons and taking advantage of some sales, Noelle felt she did a pretty good job sticking to her budget and providing her son with a good variety of Christmas gifts.

The car ride was mostly silent. James was staring out the window and Noelle, though she wondered what exactly he was thinking, didn't feel like it would be right for her to ask. Leaving it alone, she turned the radio on and allowed that to break up the silence. She appreciated the noise.

The rest of the night was similar. Libby sensed the tension in the air but didn't say too much about it. Periodically, Noelle would catch her giving her or James a curious look, but Libby never pressed for more information. She realized they had to work out their own problems and as the night wore on, she found herself more concerned about the upcoming ball and who she would end up locking lips with. That idea in itself kept her distracted from them.

Waking up early, Noelle decided to mix up some omelets. She had Christmas music playing softly and as the music was going, she was lost in a trance, mixing eggs and swaying to the music. She was in her bathrobe, hair pulled up into a ponytail so she would not get it into the food, off in her own little world.

Libby walked into the dining room area where she noticed James fixated on Noelle. Libby smiled and nudged him. James ran his hands through his hair and then rested his chin in them. He shook his head.

"Hmm?" Libby asked.

James shook his head. "She's radiant."

"Perhaps you should tell her that."

James, staring at Noelle again, didn't respond. Together, Libby and James watched as Noelle was pouring the mixture into a pan. A few moments later, with a smile on her face, oblivious to her audience, Noelle flipped the omelet, giggling because she didn't use a spatula. With ease the eggs flew in the air and landed back into the pan.

"She's skilled, too," James added quietly. He looked pained saying it. Perhaps as if he were full of regret, perhaps due to the sledding the day before. Either way, he looked like he was hurt.

"That she is," Libby agreed.

"Do you think she will ever forgive me?" he didn't look at Libby when he asked. His eyes never left his wife.

Libby had the idea that perhaps his eyes were on his wife the entire time he was gone. Was it possible that he was telling the truth, that he was really just trying to make everything work with everyone. Did he really expect that time would hold still when she left? Did he really believe he could come home and put the pieces all back together? What if the clue game didn't happen? Where would James be then? Libby wasn't sure on any of that. What she was sure on was that their mother must have seen something in him to pretty much force him back into Noelle's life. Libby thought their mom was wise to do so.

"I don't know, James. Have you asked her?" Libby realized Noelle was upset with him, but Noelle was a reasonable person. Sometimes it took her a minute to cool down, but for the most part, she would listen.

"No. I haven't," he admitted.

"Well, that's your first problem, isn't it?"

For the first time that morning, James' pulled his vision from Noelle and focused on Libby. She sensed he was studying her, reading her, to see if perhaps she was right.

"Would you have forgiven me?" James asked after a few moments.

"I'm not sure. I guess it depends on if I believed you or not. Like I said, Noelle's reasonable, but you have to be real with her."

"You're right. She can sense a lie before it ever exits someone's mouth," James stated.

"You also need to decide if you want her to forgive you."

"What do you mean?"

"James, what are your plans? Ask for forgiveness and go back to Tokyo? That isn't going to work. I know you said you were retiring, but when is that exactly? What about Levi and school? Are you wanting or even ready to move them clear across the country again? That could impact your son. Are you wanting to move back here? You need to take these things into consideration. Noelle has a life too. It's not just about you and your work. These are things that you need to think about. Maybe it's better this way. Perhaps apologize and move on. Maybe it's better if you're not together. You really need to think about what you're wanting and asking for."

"I have been. A lot."

"Well good. But please forgive me, I love this song and I need to sing now," Libby stood up and walked into the kitchen with her sister. Her voice above the radio and likely sounding better than the artist singing it, belted out the lyrics to 'Oh Holy Night'.

James shook his head and smiled. Libby was something else.

Chapter Eight
The Ball

"Noelle, can you read that clue again, so I know exactly what I'm supposed to be doing tonight?" Libby asked. She was nervously pulling her hair up.

James was already dressed and sitting on the couch waiting for the women to get ready. He was showing Levi how to make shadow monsters on the wall. Levi's big toothless smile brightened the room, relieving any tension that was there the night before.

"Here," Noelle said as she handed her sister the clue. She was curling her hair. She didn't know why, it wasn't like she was trying to meet anyone at the ball. She doubted that she would even dance. Noelle was going for the clue and the clue alone.

    LIBBY YOU'RE NEXT MY DEAR GIRL
    BEAUTIFUL BLONDE HAIR WITH THE GORGEOUS CURL
    TO THE CHRISTMAS BALL YOU THREE WILL GO
    EACH OF YOU DAZZLED UP WHITE AS THE SNOW
    MISTELTOE IS MY FAVORITE PLANT
    LIBBY STAND UNDER EACH ONE DON'T TELL ME YOU CAN'T
    HOWEVER MANY THERE ARE TWO OR EVEN THREE
    UNDER EACH ONE YOU WILL WAIT TO SEE
    WHO GOES AHEAD AND KISSES YOU
    ITS IN ONE OF THESE LEAVES YOU'LL GET YOUR NEXT CLUE
    BY THE WAY THE NIGHT IS YOUNG
    NOELLE DON'T BE A DRAG AND GO HAVE SOME FUN
    JAMES AND YOU UNDER THE MISTLETOE
    DON'T AVOID IT OR THIS I WOULD KNOW

**LEVI HAS A SITTER OF THIS I AM SURE
SHE IS THE LADY THAT LIVES NEXT DOOR**

"Why me?" Libby asked frustrated. She looked at Noelle with anxiety in her eyes. "You know this isn't safe, right?" Libby contested.

"We're right there. We won't let anything happen to you," Noelle promised.

"I hate this. I've never been that girl to stand under the mistletoe and wait for someone to approach me. It's degrading."

James walked into the dining area and laughed. "Libby, think of it this way. It gives guys who would never once take a chance, an opportunity to kiss a beautiful girl. Think of it as a help to society. You're making men's dreams come true!" he smiled and shrugged.

Libby rolled her eyes. "Joy," she replied.

Noelle walked out of the bathroom. "James is right, you know."

James looking up, glanced at Noelle. He opened his mouth to say something, but the words wouldn't come out. He was speechless. Breathless. Stunned. Noelle was dressed in a pure white gown. It was slender and hugged her at the waist. It was cut out in the back and the cut out was lined with what looked like diamond accents. Her long brown hair was half pulled up, the other half dangling in curls. Her large green eyes were bursting with color, with the help of her purple eyeshadow to bring more attention to the green.

"Noelle. You... You're lovely... beautiful... stunning." James was never at a loss for words.

"Thank you," Noelle smiled. It was a genuine smile. She liked the compliment. She looked at him dazzled in his white tux, she knew she would look good standing next to him. Frustrated or not, she knew there is nobody she would rather be seen with, especially on a night like this one.

"Just don't leave me there. I don't want a creepy person getting ahold of me!" Libby protested.

"Scouts honor," James said, saluting her.

"I promise," Noelle agreed.

After dropping Levi off to the neighbor's house (it floored Noelle how their mom prepared for everything, including the babysitter) the three showed up to the ball. Noelle thought it was funny how anxious her sister was. Nothing ever seemed to bother Libby, though today, she was fidgeting like crazy. More than once Noelle reminded her that she was fine and that she needed to chill out.

"I just can't stand the thought of a stranger's lips on me," she said.

"You'll be fine. It will be nice and easy."

"That's because you're not the one having to do it!" Libby argued back.

Noelle thought about it for a moment. She couldn't really argue that statement. There's no way she would want some random people kissing her.

Together the three of them walked into the city hall that was all decked out to hold the Christmas ball. Everything was made up in white, silver, and blue. There were silver snowflakes hanging from the ceiling. An entire nativity scene was sculpted out of ice. The Christmas tree itself was at least two stories high and decorated to go with the wintry theme.

"Let's find the mistletoe so we can get this over with," Libby grumbled.

Noelle, feeling a little less in a hurry than Libby, nodded as she made small talk with some of the parents she recognized from Levi's school.

Libby's frustration was evident when she grabbed Noelle's hand and physically pulled her toward the door. "Come on! I want to get this over with already!" she stated.

Noelle, trying to keep the peace, followed her sister toward the door. James stood back a little bit, so he wasn't the one forced to kiss Libby, which could have been totally awkward. He wanted to be close enough to protect her if someone decided to be a little too interested.

Finding the mistletoe right away, Libby reluctantly stood there. Her expression as if she just bit into a lemon, made for a really difficult approach by any guy.

"Fix your face or you're going to be standing here forever!" Noelle scolded her sister.

"I hate this!" Libby moaned.

"I know. But you said, rules are rules and we're to abide by them. Remember?"

"Yeah, yeah. Well, I guess you might as well make yourself useful while I'm standing here and start digging through this disgusting plant to look for Mom's next clue," Libby suggested sarcastically.

"I can't. You need to be kissed first. No guy is going to approach you while I'm standing above your head searching through the mistletoe. That would be absurd."

"I hate this!" Libby whined again.

"I know. Just smile so you can get it over with."

Libby obeyed. Noelle stood about four feet from her sister and leaned up against the wall. She didn't want to deter anyone from kissing her, however, she didn't want to leave her alone either.

Once Libby changed her face, it took no time at all for an elderly gentleman to show up and plant one on Libby's cheek. Libby smiled and thanked him. The two made small talk for a few minutes. The gentleman laughed, explaining to Libby that this was the most action he's had over the past decade. Libby giggled.

Noelle smiled at her sister. She was handling this like a champ. For as nervous as Libby was, she handled the little peck like a pro. Noelle had secretly hoped some good-looking guy would woo Libby, sweeping her off her feet. Libby has been single for over a year now, and didn't seem to mind, but secretly Noelle knew Libby was a little lonely. She enjoyed having the company of a guy with her, especially one who enjoyed going on adventures and long road trips with her. Libby loved doing those types of things and since being single, she's enjoyed a few trips alone. As much as she's appreciated them, it's always better with a partner.

James watched the interaction between Libby and the older guy. His heart warmed when he saw his sister-in-law smile and converse with the old man, having all the weirdness and discomfort of her situation leave her. He felt a sense of pride. James has always looked at Libby as a younger sister. Watching her, he missed what it was like to be a part of the family. He was grateful to be there with them, but it wasn't the same. He didn't realize how much things could change in three years. When people say that time flies, they're not kidding. For James, time actually flew. He had wanted so badly to give Noelle the life she deserved, and he was so focused on it that he forgot to pay attention to what was actually important. Watching Noelle interact with Libby gave him that reminder of how imperative it is to spend quality time with family. If he could hit the rewind button, he would have done things so differently. He quietly wondered to himself if it was too late, or if he would be granted another chance.

As soon as the elderly man left, Noelle high-fived Libby. She was proud of her sister for dealing with the transaction with so much grace. After the elderly man was gone, Noelle checked to make sure nobody was really paying attention to them. Seeing that the coast was clear, she quickly fumbled around with the mistletoe in hopes of finding the next clue. She wasn't surprised when it wasn't there. She knew it couldn't be that easy.

Together the three of them set off to try and find the next mistletoe. It took a few minutes because there was a line at the other door, but they assumed based on all the people ducking down to kiss, that there was one there.

"Let's get this done with," Libby said as she made her way toward the doorway.

"Libby, what are you going to do cut in front of everyone in line just to stand under the mistletoe? That doesn't make sense," Noelle had a valid point.

"I say let it clear some. In the mean while we can have a bite to eat, or dance, or something," James suggested.

Libby reluctantly agreed. "I just want to get this done with," Libby replied.

"Yes, but we want to be inconspicuous too, don't we?" James asked.

"I guess," Libby agreed.

"Look guys, they have a photo booth!" Noelle pointed excitedly.

Libby rolled her eyes. In her mind, this day couldn't end fast enough. Regardless, she reluctantly agreed to take some pictures with her sister and brother-in-law. The three of them squeezed in the booth the best way they could. They made faces at the camera, they smiled, they posed, and it didn't take long before they were all laughing together, including Libby.

After they walked around for a bit, Noelle realized that the room was a lot more crowded than it had been. She glanced toward the other entrance to see if the line died down and sure enough, there were just a few people standing around, but nobody really in line trying to come in.

"Libby, now's your chance!" Noelle encouraged her sister.

Feeling the anxiety rise in her stomach, she reluctantly made her way toward the door. She silently asked her mother why she had to do this to her, but she knew her mother was fine with the idea and wasn't going to respond anyway. She took a deep breath, slapped a smile on her face, and stood under the mistletoe. James and Noelle stood a few feet away, pretending not to be paying attention, but really watching Libby like a hawk.

In a matter of seconds, a big guy around his early 50's licked his lips aggressively and rubbed his hands together. He looked at Libby like she was a juicy ribeye steak. James cringed at the idea of this guy touching his sister-in-law and just as he was about to dive in and rescue her, another guy in a white tux swooped in and very quickly yet wistfully, kissed Libby gently on the lips.

"Sorry, I hope I didn't scare you. There's no way I was going to let you get eaten up by him," her savior said of the large fella.

"No, thank you. I appreciate it," Libby replied. She had a faint smile trace her lips.

Noelle, saw the spark in her eye and grinned. She knew immediately that Libby was kind of liking this guy.

The larger fella was still approaching Libby who was standing under the mistletoe with the guy in the white tuxedo.

"What's your name?" Libby asked him, not noticing the beastly guy who was fast approaching.

"My name's Nate. Come on, you need to get out from under here. I'm scared that guy's going to eat you."

Libby obeyed, without the speck of a worry on her face. Noelle was so focused on Libby and her beau and solving the clues that she wasn't thinking about the fact that she was now standing under the mistletoe. She was so absorbed in searching the mistletoe, that it didn't really dawn on her when somebody grabbed her by the shoulder.

"Hang on, I'm trying to find the clue," she said.

She only realized what was happening when she heard James say, "Not so fast buddy, she's mine!"

Noelle glanced over her shoulder and was startled to see the guy standing directly behind her. She jumped and James grabbed ahold of her, kissing her fiercely and passionately. The other guy grunted and walked away.

"Man, he was something else!" James said, still hanging onto Noelle.

"Thank you for that." Noelle replied. She felt slightly embarrassed. "I guess I was so busy paying attention to Libby and the clue that I forgot to take care of myself," she added.

"I'm glad you're okay," James agreed. He took a deep breath, catching his bearings and then asked, "still no clue?"

Noelle shook her head. She couldn't find one anyway. "Libby's busy with Nate, do you want to take a walk and see if we can find anymore mistletoe?"

"Yeah, I supposed. Should you warn your sister first, just in case she wants an escape plan?"

"Yeah, we can let her know, but I think she won't care. She seems to be... preoccupied," Noelle said with a smile.

James laughed. "Funny how things change, isn't it?"

Noelle nodded. She approached her sister while she admired how animated Libby gets when she's comfortable with people. Noelle could tell that Nate was someone Libby was hitting it off with well.

"Sis, we're going to look around for more mistletoe. You can either join us, or we'll come find you in a few," Noelle said.

"You guys go ahead. I'll be around here somewhere when you find it," Libby grinned.

Noelle nodded. She walked away with James trailing behind her.

"You guys are on a mistletoe hunt, huh?" Nate asked grinning.

"Kind of. It's a long story, but basically my mom kind of set up this thing where we have to solve clues to get to the next clue, almost like a scavenger hunt. She passed away 7 months ago, this was like her last hoorah for us before she went..." Libby trailed off. She hated to think about her mom being gone. To snap herself out of the funk she looked at Nate and grinned. She admired how he looked in his tux. He, too, had blonde hair and blue eyes. He was strong looking, had a nice jaw line and broad shoulders. He smelled good, but had a quiet humility about him. He wasn't by any means flashy or loud. He seemed to be a subtle guy. He had manners and spoke well of his family. Libby liked that in a guy. He didn't appear to be unsure of himself or weak, either.

"I'm sorry for your loss," he said.

"Thank you."

"Would you like to dance?"

"I thought you would never ask," Libby smiled.

Noelle and James continued on their journey searching the entire place for mistletoe. Aside from the two entrances, they couldn't figure out where else may hang one. Noelle looked near where they were serving food and beverages, but nothing was there. James checked by where the food was prepared, the little kitchenette area, but he didn't see anything there either. They looked around for a backdoor or emergency exit, but they weren't able to find anything.

"Are you sure you checked both plants thoroughly?" James asked, getting ready to give up.

"Yes, it's not like mistletoe is thick or large or anything. It's a squirrely kind of plant. I don't know how she would have hidden a clue in one anyway."

"Is it a trick like some of the other clues were? I mean, is there a sign with a picture of mistletoe on it, or Christmas wrap, or anything like that?" James asked thoughtfully.

"Your guess is as good as mine."

The two searched high and low for any signs of mistletoe that they could find.

"Isn't it poison?" James, asked out of the blue.

"What's poison?"

"Mistletoe, isn't it poison?"

"Sure is. It's also a parasite if you think about it," Noelle laughed. "Truthfully, it's more like a nuisance weed."

James shook his head with a smile. "I kind of like that weed," he admitted.

"Yeah?"

"Well, it made it so I could kiss you tonight," James stopped and looked at Noelle.

Her face reddened. "Come on, we need to be finding this clue."

Noelle's brain had a hard time searching for mistletoe. It was repeating James' words over and over again. She knew he would have said more if she wouldn't have cut him off. She wanted to hear more, which made her wonder why she did cut him off. She figured now wasn't the time. She needed to be alone with him to talk about these sorts of things. She didn't want to risk feeling emotional at the ball in front of people.

Noelle had a good idea. She figured she could ask someone who decorated the place where they hung the mistletoe. She started to look around for people wearing nametags. They were the ones who put the ball together and they were wearing nametags in case something went wrong, they were easily identified. Noelle walked up to the first person she saw. It was an elderly lady wearing a red dress.

"Excuse me, ma'am," Noelle started.

"Yes?"

"Um, could you tell me where you guys hung all your mistletoe?"

The lady looked at Noelle and then at James and a huge smile spread across her face. She leaned in and told Noelle, "I can't blame you one bit for wanting to get under the mistletoe with him. He's a handsome fella now isn't he, dear?"

Noelle blushed. "He is. But that's not really the reason I was looking for it."

"Well, both entrances have mistletoe, get your smooch under one of them."

"Yes, I looked at those ones, I was wondering if there were any other places you guys hung it?" Noelle asked.

"Ahh, you're looking for more privacy?" The lady gave Noelle an exaggerated wink.

Noelle blushed again. She felt ridiculous and yet, she didn't want to explain the situation either. She just shrugged.

"I think there was some out in the hallway near the bathrooms," the elderly lady winked at Noelle again.

"Thank you, so much!"

Noelle and James walked off the dancefloor and into the hallway. They were stopped by an usher as they were headed out the door.

"You two just went under the mistletoe. You need to kiss her quickly before I do!" he grinned at James.

James obliged. He kissed Noelle softly on the lips. They both could feel the sparks, but they didn't have time for that right then. The doorman beamed. "Don't you just love Christmas?" he asked.

"I really do," James answered with a chuckle.

Together, Noelle and James searched the hallway and near the bathrooms. "I'm not seeing anything, are you?" She asked, frustrated.

"No, Noey, I really don't..."

"What?"

"Nothing... it's just that... I was wondering what if your mom's clue was found by someone else, or perhaps they didn't hang that piece of the mistletoe that she had it stuck in. I hate to go there, but I can't help but think that it's a possibility."

"I thought that too," Noelle admitted. "But I can't accept that. My mom has pulled this off, to the point the neighbor reminded us this morning that she was babysitting. There's no way my mom would have missed a detail like that."

"I hope not," James replied sounding less sure.

They searched the hallway and into both of the bathrooms. Nothing. Giving up, they decided to find Libby and let her know they were out of ideas. They walked through the ball and as they tried to shuffle through the crowd of people, their wedding song came on.

"One dance, and then we find Libby?" James asked.

Noelle hesitated. James was persistent. He reached for her hand and lead her to the dance floor. The Four Tops were singing, 'I believe in you and me.' James quietly sang along with the song. He looked at Noelle and smiled. "I miss us," he said.

"I missed us too. That's why I left. James, you chose to be gone all the time," Noelle didn't want this conversation right now. She didn't want her heart to be trampled on. She didn't want to argue.

"You're right, Noey. I made a mistake. I hope you can forgive me. I am truly sorry for ever hurting you and especially for neglecting you and Levi. You own my heart and you always will."

Noelle had to struggle to keep her balance. She had waited for three years to hear an apology from him. She had been bitter and angry that she never received it. That he never chased after her, never fought for their marriage. Yet, here he was. Was it better late than never? She wondered what would have happened if her mom didn't put the clues together. Would he have ever apologized then? She wanted to know. She wanted to ask him. But she couldn't. Not now. Not yet.

"I can start to forgive you. I just have so many unanswered questions," Noelle stated.

"I will spend the rest of our lives answering every question if you allow me."

Noelle looked at him. She could tell he meant his words. He was looking at her directly in the eye. She didn't know what to say. She wanted more than anything to say everything was okay and that of course they would be happily together in their very own version of 'happily ever after,' but she still had questions.

"I have questions. Lots of them. We'll talk and then we'll decide."

"Noelle, I can't wat until after Christmas anymore. This is getting to be too hard. I know it's hard, but can we please make time before Christmas. Just me and you. I will be honest and tell you everything, but I am asking if we can please do this sooner than later."

Noelle thought about it. She thought about what would happen if she hated his explanation and then Christmas would be ruined. She understood where he was coming from. Christmas could be ruined regardless. If neither party knew what was going on then that could make for a very awkward Christmas. Especially considering Levi could start to become very confused, probably more than what he already is.

"Okay. We can talk before hand on one condition…"

"Anything."

"No matter what happens. No matter what we decide. You must stay through Christmas for Levi's sake. I can't stand the idea of his heart being broken. That's the only way."

"I promise. If you hate me, I will still stay and make Christmas with Levi special."

Noelle took a deep breath. She knew he was being honest. James was never a good liar, so she didn't even consider not believing him.

James pulled Noelle's head toward him. He wrapped his arms around her and held her close as their wedding song played. Noelle, head on James' chest, listened to the rhythm of his heart. She remembered how many nights she would lay on him and the soft tempo of his heart would lull her to sleep. This was a rhythm she could never forget, essentially music to her ears.

Captured in a full embrace, dancing to the song they swore described their feelings for each other, years ago. Full of hurt and pain, but also feeling totally at peace and in harmony, the couple molded together, united as one. Noelle felt the familiar strength of him protecting her in a way nobody ever could. It was ironic to her that she recognized his movements and how familiar they felt after three years of being apart.

The song finished. Noelle felt awkward as she struggled to decide if she should continue to hold onto James or to let him go. She glanced up at him who also appeared to struggle with what to do. Neither appeared to be ready to let go of the other one. James made the first move.

"We need to find Libby so we can decide what we're going to do about this mistletoe situation."

"That sounds like a great movie. 'The Mistletoe Mission,'" Noelle laughed.

James smiled. "You're a dork," he said lovingly.

"That's probably true," Noelle winked at him and lead the way to find Libby.

Moments later they spotted Libby, who was still with Nate, sitting at a round table, laughing hysterically.

Nate had a huge smile on his face and when Noelle and James approached, Nate stood to greet them.

Noelle, grinning, explained to Libby that they had no idea where another mistletoe could possibly be. She explained that they need to come to a decision or else they would miss this clue, stopping the entire thing from moving forward.

Libby shook her head. Noelle gave her a confused look.

"I have the clue right here," she explained.

"How'd you find it?" Noelle asked.

"Well, while you two lovebirds were lost in each other's arms, me and Nate here, decided to go on a search for the missing mistletoe..."

"Hey that makes for a pretty great movie title too!" James laughed.

"... Anyway, the only place we could think to search that you may not have looked was on the Christmas tree. Which might I add is covered in mistletoe!"

"Yeah, you should have seen how many times me and Libby had to kiss just to get the guy to let us check for the clue!" Nate laughed.

"I wouldn't have minded having that problem," James said giving Noelle a sideways glance.

Noelle gave him a quick smack on the arm. "James!" She scolded.

James shrugged. He winked at Nate and shook his head.

"So you have the clue. What does it say?" Noelle asked eagerly.

"I don't know Noelle, this one's kind of different."

"Let's hear it."

IF A+B=C
AND 1+2=3
USING THE EQUATION TO SOLVE THIS
S-A-N-T-A IS THE ADDRESS
ON A STREET THAT IS FUN
IF YOU GET THE WRONG HOUSE YOU MAY WANT TO RUN
SEARCH HIGH AND LOW THIS CLUE WILL BE HARD TO SEE
I'LL GIVE YOU A HINT IT'S BY THE 'B'

"This does sound hard," Noelle agreed.

"That's what I thought. It's going to be tricky, but I'm a little concerned about walking through someone's yard."

"Right. Like what street is fun?" James wondered out loud.

Noelle and Libby looked at him and shook their heads. They had no idea what their mom was getting at either.

"I mean, is it fun like a bumpy road with lots of turns? Or is it fun by title, for example like 'Scooter St.'?" Libby asked.

"This is going to be a big task tomorrow," Noelle agreed.

"Like the mistletoe mission?" James laughed.

Libby looked at him funnily.

"He's just being a nerd," Noelle explained.

"Perhaps, but you're the dork," James replied laughing.

Noelle rolled her eyes. Her smirk made her annoyance less convincing. Everyone laughed. As they got ready to call it a night, James and Noelle allowed Libby and Nate a few moments while they walked toward the car.

"Will I see you again?" Nate asked.

"Perhaps," Libby said with a smile.

"I'll plan on it then."

"You're pretty confident for just getting to know me."

"Not confident, I just know what I'm looking for and I am pretty sure you're it."

"How do you know that I think the same about you?"

"I don't. I just have to have faith," Nate winked at her and then grabbed her hand gently kissing it good-bye.

"Faith?"

"Yeah. Faith. I believe that things happen for a reason. I stumbled across you, saving you from some strange guy, while you happen to be under a mistletoe. That's some movie stuff right there. It's magic."

"You don't think that it just randomly happened like that?"

"Nope. It was too perfect to be a coincidence. Have a good night, Libby."

"Night." Libby walked toward the car feeling a bit of confusion mixed with a lot of excitement. The truth was, she really liked Nate. She just wondered if she would feel the same way tomorrow. With her track record, she would likely ignore his calls and keep going solo. She was comfortable that way, regardless if she was lonely or not. Even though Libby was only working part time, nursing was a pretty demanding job. Add singing events on the weekends, she wasn't sure she had the time to really date anyone anyway. She shook her head trying to convince herself that a relationship was exactly what she didn't need, something inside of her was tugging at her to reconsider and actually get to know Nate. She found herself struggling pretty hard to ignore that voice.

Chapter Nine
The Street that is Fun

Noelle, in her usual fashion, woke up early that morning to cook breakfast. She had the music on just loud enough for her to hear and not disturb the others. She fried the potatoes and added some chunks of ham, green peppers, mushrooms, and cheese, making a breakfast casserole. She swayed her hips to the music as she was starting to really feel like she was in the Christmas spirit for the first time this year. It was an exciting feeling.

Noelle always felt her best when her hair was pulled up on top of her head and she was at the stove. The fluffy snowflakes coming from Lake Michigan only made her that much more at peace. She smiled as she placed some homemade cinnamon rolls into the oven. She knew once they started to bake that nobody would continue sleep. There is nothing like the smell of cinnamon and sugar permeating through a home. It's those types of things that Noelle decided actually turned a building into a home. She absolutely loved it.

Just as she had assumed, as soon as the cinnamon rolls started to rise, everyone started to stir. In no time, her family was sitting at the dining room table, everyone with a smile on their face. Noelle beamed as she put the icing on the rolls and then served the casserole. Watching everyone wide eyed as she served them their breakfast made her long for her own restaurant even more than she had been. Though the idea was silly, Noelle wondered if she could ever pull it off. She didn't want it to be big and fancy, just a small little restaurant and bakery would be perfect for her. A few menu items with different specials and new things to try every day. Something casual like she was.

Realizing that she was in reality and in reality, there are bills to pay and jobs to do, Noelle snapped herself out of her own little fantasy. She took a deep breath and realized that she could be grateful for the few that get to taste her ideas right there with her. She was still a cook regardless if she could afford a restaurant or not. She could accept that, even though deep down if money wasn't an issue, she would be serving far more people. One day... she promised herself this to keep herself going. For now, she grinned as she heard the mmmm's and ahhhh's of her loved ones. She laughed when Levi asked to lick the plate that the rolls were on. Hearing that, her heart was full. Christmas was going to be okay after all.

When everyone finished up and rinsed their plates, took a shower, and did all the other morning routines, Noelle had everyone gather at the table. "We need to figure out the street that is fun," she explained.

"I've been thinking of that all night long," Libby agreed.

"I can google every street in the city to help us break it down some-" James started.

"-No!" The girls stopped him quickly. They both glanced up toward the ceiling as if to make sure their mother wasn't watching them; or that there weren't some secret cameras hiding in a corner somewhere.

"Sorry. I forgot," James said, holding his hands up as if he were just caught red-handed.

"No, that's fine, it's just that she keeps saying she would know if we did something wrong. It's kind of strange," Noelle explained.

James nodded in agreement. "So, what's a better way we can do this?" he asked.

Everyone sat around the table with a blank expression on their face.

"I know," Levi said.

The adults looked at him and smiled. "Okay, Levi, what's your idea?"

"We could go to the bank. They got that train set and the whole city is on there. The one that grandma would give me the quarter to make the train drive around the tracks just like it does outside," Levi explained.

The adults looked at him with awe. "Levi, that's a great idea!" James said.

Immediately everyone stood up at the same time and grabbed their coats. "Come on, we have a mission. Libby can you grab a pen and paper? Levi you can help us find every fun street. This was truly an awesome idea!" Noelle rubbed her son's curls. She admired herself for raising such a bright young man.

Dressed in snow gear, prepared for whatever type of mission they were going on, the four of them walked together into the city bank. Though they looked a little awkward standing around the gigantic train set, nobody seemed to think too much about them. The small street signs were a little tough to read, but they were able to make them out for the most part. The entire town was represented in the train set. Obviously, not every house and building were in there, however they had enough that you could figure out exactly where you were at. Every street was accounted for.

"Okay, fun streets," Libby stated as she stared at the town in front of her.

"Let's start with names," Noelle recommended.

"There are a few roads in there that look twisty and curvy," James pointed out.

"Do you guys think it matters that mom said, 'street'"? Noelle asked. "Like was she being literal or could street mean road, boulevard, avenue, etc.?"

"At this point lets take everything into consideration. I will write them down in categories. I will place each 'fun' sounding name in a list under a subcategory of street, avenue, etc. I will also have a category for 'fun' looking streets. That way we can start literal, but we have everything accounted for," Libby said, realizing this was going to be a much bigger task than she realized.

"That makes sense," James agreed.

"Levi, you came up with the idea; were there any streets you and grandma would call fun, specifically?" Noelle was hoping Levi could make this a lot easier.

"I don't think so," Levi replied.

Libby wasn't looking for streets. She was busy enough trying to keep up with what Noelle, James, and Levi were telling her to write down. She was a good note-taker and she would check to verify that each street they came up with went under the right category. She considered color-coded them but decided that could be a little too confusing, especially because she was cross-referencing some. She settled on keeping her lists and putting stars around streets that accounted for multiple categories.

After about an hour, they ran out of ideas of 'fun' streets. Libby looked at her list. She had 17 street names that could be considered 'fun'. She had 9 'fun' streets in regard to construction or drivability. She felt good about her list, but she wondered if this was the right track. She was reminded of when she was younger, and their mom would take them for a drive to look at the Christmas lights. Libby remembered some of the streets that were extremely well lit, she would consider those the 'fun streets to go on.' She had a hunch that nothing on her list was going to make the cut.

"Noelle, I just came to a random realization," she stated, staring at the list.

"That none of the streets with the fun names are the ones we would enjoy going to as kids?" Noelle asked, reading her mind.

"How'd you know?"

"It just dawned on me a couple of minutes ago."

"Do you think Mom was referring to the streets that were all lit up that we would beg her to take us by?"

"Libs, I have no idea. Maybe?" Noelle was starting to feel her anxiety as Christmas was nearing and they had no idea how many more clues they had to go to fulfill their mother's final wish.

"Do you think the address thing is a clue to help us figure out the street?" James chimed in.

"I'm open to trying anything," Noelle replied.

It was then, after an hour of time spent in the bank, that a police officer approached them.

"You guys have been in here for a while. This is a place of business and the bank manager asked me to move you along."

"Sorry officer, we were just going through the city with my son. We didn't mean to cause any problems. We were just getting ready to leave, anyway," Noelle stated. She looked at the cop and blushed. She didn't expect him to be as good looking as he was.

"Well, I hope that you have a good day and a Merry Christmas," he said.

"Evan? Evan Parker, right?" James asked smiling.

"Yeah, that's right. Oh, my goodness! James Miller? Man, it's been years! How are you doing?"

Noelle watched in awe as James and the police officer hugged. They were chit-chatting for a moment. Noelle glanced up at the bank manager who seemed upset that they were standing there even longer, this time with a cop, that she couldn't help but grin.

James filled Officer Evan Parker in on the details regarding the Christmas clues and their search for a 'fun street'. According to Officer Parker, the street that he thinks is the most fun is the one that is for bikes only. No cars are allowed on the street, but it's an actual street. It has ramps and hills and things like that for people on bicycles, skateboards, etc. The state was trying to endorse healthy lifestyle choices so they put a few of these streets up in hopes that people would ride on them, saving motor emissions and also helping people to exercise. Either way, there are addresses and everything on these streets.

James thought that was an interesting idea and agreed to check out those streets as well. The officer brought them back to the train set to show them where these types of streets are located. Libby wrote down the information and was happy to see that at the bank, they were in a pretty centralized location for pretty much every street they wanted to look at.

Officer Parker answered some code on his walkie talkie and then told them that they all better get going. He explained to the manager that there was no harm being planned against his bank that they were just trying to map out the city for a game. The bank manager seemed to calm down some, but the officer advised them that it would be best if they left anyway. He shook James' hand and gave him a half of hug and then followed them out of the door.

"That was interesting," Libby remarked.

"Mom, we almost went to jail!" Levi said excitedly.

"No, we didn't. He was just making sure everything was okay," Noelle corrected him.

"He was good-looking too!" Libby chimed in from nowhere.

Noelle nodded. James shook his head. They all laughed.

"So, where should we start?" Noelle asked, wanting to get back to the clue. They didn't have a lot of daytime hours to work with.

"Let's figure out the house numbers. I feel that could be helpful," James suggested.

"I need to see the clue again," Libby said.

Noelle handed it to her.

IF A+B=C
AND 1+2=3
USING THE EQUATION TO SOLVE THIS
S-A-N-T-A IS THE ADDRESS
ON A STREET THAT IS FUN
IF YOU GET THE WRONG HOUSE YOU MAY WANT TO RUN
SEARCH HIGH AND LOW THIS CLUE WILL BE HARD TO SEE
I'LL GIVE YOU A HINT IT'S BY THE 'B'

"I don't get it," Noelle admitted as she looked at the equation.

"That's because it's math. You never get math. It's like you see numbers and decide to give up. This is a piece of cake, Noelle, and trust me, I know you get cake," Libby smiled.

"I don't give up when I see numbers in a recipe," Noelle reminded her.

"Ha! Yes, you do! That's why you refuse to use recipes and just make your own!" Libby laughed.

Noelle nodded. "I didn't think about that," Noelle agreed. "I guess it just doesn't make sense to me. There are no numbers on letters. It's too algebraic," Noelle complained.

"Mom, it's for kindergarteners! I would have done this last year! If C is 3 how many beans does one and two have?

That's easy. We learned there's 26 letters in the alphabet. If C is three it makes sense that A the first letter is one. And B the second letter is two. All the way down to 26," Levi looked at his mother as if she had a salamander doing a curtsey on her head. "You taught me this stuff, Mom!" Levi laughed.

"Is that all it is?" Noelle asked James and Libby.

They both nodded their heads. "Looks like Levi has it right," Libby smiled and high-fived her nephew.

"So, do we add it at the end? Or just let it be the numbers?" Noelle asked.

"That's what I want to figure out. If we don't add it then it would be a really long address, but that may be what gives us the answer we need," James replied.

"Okay, using Levi's methodology, we have to figure out the numbers for each letter for SANTA," Libby reiterated. "S-19, A-1, N-14, T-20, A-1... right?"

"So you're trying to tell me that the address is 19114201 on some kind of 'Fun' Street?"

"That doesn't seem right, does it?" James stated feeling a little defeated. Out of all the clues, this one seemed to be the toughest, he thought.

"I'm at a loss..." Noelle stated feeling a little let down. She wanted to solve the clues just right, but this clue was by far the most difficult. Her mom was an outside of the box type of thinker, but this clue was simply hard. Nobody had an address that was that long. How were they going to figure this out?

"We could forget about the address for now and start looking up and down the streets we have written down. See if anything triggers an 'aha' type of reaction. Or perhaps one matches the address in some sort of way, or maybe we get lucky and find the 'B' she was talking about. What do you guys think?" Libby was trying to stay optimistic.

"What other choice do we have?" Noelle piped in.

"We really have nothing to lose. I'm game," James agreed.

The four of them all on the same mission driving up and down the streets on the list, doing anything they could to solve this clue. Levi was infatuated with the yard decorations. He was excited to point them out to his parents as they drove past each house. They drove for at least an hour, perhaps longer, before Noelle heard Levi's stomach growling. She glanced at the clock and realized it was already hitting one o'clock. Levi hadn't eaten lunch yet. Noelle made the executive decision to stop their drive and to go sit down with the clues in a restaurant so they could all eat. Perhaps it would be easier to solve the clue this way.

Moments later, the four of them were sitting at a table, working on numbers puzzles in order to try and figure out what their mother was trying to get them to figure out. While Levi ate his grilled cheese sandwich and french-fries, the adults barely touched their food, trying to solve the clue. Suddenly, the look on Libby's face changed.

"What is it?" Noelle asked, seeing that Libby had what looked like a lightbulb go off.

"Okay, so in the clue, Mom reversed it. She said, 'If A+B=C and 1+2=3'. If we take the numbers of SANTA, 19114201 and turn the address to a typical sized address... that would be three, four, or five numbers, then we use the rests of the numbers and turn them into letters..."

"...Wouldn't that just be the end of the letters of SANTA? So, TA or NTA?" Noelle asked frustrated.

"Not necessarily. Because the numbers are double digits. For example, there's no 42 in the alphabet. But there is a 4 and a 2..."

"This makes no sense," Noelle shook her head and then took a bite of her fry.

"Wait. Libby may be on to something. Is there any way that the last numbers spell a street that happens to be on our list?" James asked.

"Let's see..." Libby grabbed the pen and her list. She was bound and determined to figure this out.

"Okay, if the address is 191, that leaves us with... 14201. That could be a few things...

NTA (14+20+1)

ADBA (1+4+2+1)

NBA (14+2+1)

Make sense?" Libby looked around the table.

Noelle seemed to be interested but also confused. It was apparent that she didn't like this clue. James appeared to be more intrigued.

"Let's try it again if it's 1911," he said.

"Okay that would leave us with 4201," Libby stated.

"DTA (4+20+1)

DU (4+21)

I think that's it for that one," Libby said.

"Okay, let's try and do it as a five-digit address."

"Okay, that leaves us with 201.

BA (2+1)

TA (20+1)." Libby set her pen down and grabbed her notes.

"Libs, do any of these names match a street on the list?" James asked eagerly. He thought one sounded familiar, but he didn't want to give his hopes up.

Before Libby could answer the waitress stopped at their table. She asked if they needed anything else and refilled everyone's pop. Libby was waiting anxiously for her to leave. She placed her hand over her cup and said that she was fine. After refusing dessert three times, the waitress finally left the bill on the table and walked away. James quickly grabbed the bill before anyone noticed.

"I thought she'd never leave!" Libby exclaimed. She grabbed her notepad and started to read through her lists of streets.

"Any match?" Noelle asked.

"Um, actually strangely enough, two of them do," Libby replied. She grabbed her pen and scribbled down the two streets that matched. Adba and Ta.

"Adba and Ta? You guys have some funny street names around here," James remarked.

"I say we try these two streets first and we will look to see if the address matches either of the streets. Upon finding the address we will check both streets for a 'B'. Does that sound like a plan?" Libby was excited and everyone could tell. She felt like this clue was the hardest and to have some headway on it because of her idea gave her a sense of pride.

Noelle nodded. "I think that makes the most sense," she said, agreeing. "I couldn't have come close to solving this one," she added.

"We all have different strengths," James added. "That's what makes us a great team."

Libby smiled at James as she looked at Noelle. She didn't know what was going to happen with the two of them, but she hoped that they would get back together. They were always such a great couple. Libby doesn't blame Noelle for leaving him, she would have too, but Libby also knew that James was a good guy and that everyone deserved a break once in a while.

Noelle didn't say anything, but now that they had the clue making a little more sense, she soon found herself ready to actually eat her food instead of just pick at it. It seemed that was the same feeling Libby and James had as well, because in no time at all the table was quiet and everyone was eating. Which was right about the time Levi was finishing his plate.

"It's going to be on Ta street," Levi stated matter-of-factly.

"Why do you say that?" Noelle asked curiously.

"Because I never heard of the other one. And me and granny used to drive on Ta Street to get to the jump house. That was always fun," Levi explained.

"That solves it!" James exclaimed. "We'll go down Ta first."

Libby and Noelle nodded as they finished their sandwiches.

"I'll meet you guys out in the car. I need to use the phone right quick," James informed them.

Before they could object, he got up, paid the bill, and walked out to the car. Noelle was watching him as he leaned up against the hood talking into his cell phone. She could tell by looking at him that he was talking business. It was strange to her how she remembered so clearly every little detail about him, even though it's been years since she's even seen him. The way he talked, so professional, so confident, was beautiful to her. But she also remembered the long hours, the business trips that often went over. There was no way she could deal with that again. Granted, it was nice to spend this time with him and his attention has been mostly undivided, she still carries the pain from the past and doesn't want to experience the hurt again. She realized after watching him laugh into the phone that she and James would likely never be again. However, as she promised, she would talk to him before Christmas and she and he would share Christmas together this last time for Levi.

Libby noticed Noelle's demeanor change. "Don't even think about it!" she scolded her sister. "You don't know what he's doing, you haven't even talked to him or given him a chance yet."

Noelle shrugged. "History repeats itself."

"Not if you or another person does something to change it, to prevent it from happening again," Libby stated.

Noelle shook her head. "I told him we'd talk about it. We will. That's all I can promise."

Libby took a drink of her pop and then placed the cup on the table. "Let's get going on this clue," she stated, intentionally changing the subject.

By the time they made it out the door, it took a couple of extra minutes because they didn't realize James already had the check taken care of, they approached the car only to hear James telling someone that he needed to go. Noelle thought it was amazing how much deeper his voice would get when he was on the phone for business. She thought about it and she realized it was the same for her, only her voice became higher and kind of squeaky.

Noelle drove the team to Ta Street. Admittedly, she had to agree with James, she thought these street names were quite absurd. Regardless, they had only about three hours of daylight left. They needed to locate the address and look for something regarding to a 'B'. The thought of the 'B' made her nervous because her mother actually had it typed in quotes. She didn't do that for the rest of the clues so far. This clue was already the hardest one by a landslide. She wondered if that meant the next clue would be even trickier. She hoped not. She wondered how many clues they had to go before they were able to solve the riddle. Part of her hoped that there would be a lot more left, she kind of enjoyed feeling her mother's presence with them. The other part hoped that they were finishing soon. She was starting to get curious to see what all this was about.

"What was the address we were looking for?" Noelle asked as she drove down the street.

"19114," Libby replied.

"Too bad we couldn't GPS it," Noelle stated as she drove. She was currently in the 300 block of Ta. That means they had a long ways to go if it goes up into five digits.

"Just drive, we'll find it," Libby seemed quite sure of herself.

"There's a lot of traffic coming up ahead," Noelle stated.

"Do you want to turn around?" James asked.

"No, we're getting closer to where the address should be."

Noelle glanced into the rearview mirror. Her heart almost melted when she saw that James and Levi were holding hands and pointing out houses and decorations to each other. It never dawned on her how much her son missed his dad. Noelle could feel her eyes start to well up. She realized that so many kids out there don't have a dad for a variety of reasons, even though James has been out of the country for a lot of the time, he had always made it a point to call and talk to Levi, send him letters and gifts, etc. Levi actually knew his father and had a relationship with him, even though the relationship was a different kind of one. These moments were simply making up for the lost physical time and to Noelle, that was a beautiful thing.

Noelle continued down Ta Street and as she got closer to where the address should be, cars were stopped throughout the street. Traffic was quite a bit heavier. People were getting out of their cars to walk around. Curiosity got the best of Noelle so she parked about a block away and decided she wanted to see what the fuss was all about. She asked everyone if they wanted to join her or stay in the car and wait.

"We're looking for the clue anyway, right?" James asked.

Noelle nodded her head. She had momentarily forgotten about the clue when she wanted to see what was going on with traffic. She knew something was happening. "Yeah, I was just going to check out the reason for the sudden chaos, but you're right, we're right down the street from the address, we can go check it out and see if we can find the clue."

They all got out of the car. James told Levi to hold his hand and not let go because of the traffic. Levi obeyed. Noelle lead the way toward the address they were looking for. The closer they came to the address the more traffic they were running into. "Do you think it's a Christmas party of some sort?" she finally asked.

"I don't think so. It's like stop and go. People coming and going. It's weird," Libby said. She had a confused look on her face.

As they walked, houses were extravagantly decorated for Christmas. Some were fun, some were soft and almost angelic, they were all beautiful. Noelle tucked her hands into her pockets and smiled as she wandered down the road. Big houses with pillars holding them up, huge picture windows, Victorian style houses with two-story tall Christmas trees standing next to winding staircases, all of them more amazing than the last. Noelle could picture people working on their manicured lawns every summer and waving to the neighbor next door as they stood in the driveway with a bathrobe on. The thought made her giggle. Noelle could definitely see herself in this neighborhood.

They walked up the sidewalk and could hear some music playing. A few houses down, Noelle realized where the music was coming from. It just so happened to be the same address they were looking for. Which also happened to be what all the traffic and commotion was about. Noelle finally understood.

As they neared the house, everything made sense. It was a three-story, multi-colored brick home full of windows. It had a mosaic tile path leading to the front porch. The front yard was large enough to fit another house, even possibly a brownstone in front of the original home. There were shutters on every window and had it been summer, Noelle could see where the exotic plants would have been sitting. Being almost Christmas, instead of the flowers, there were an abundance of decorations taking their place. Decorations that had to have been custom made. Noelle hasn't ever seen decorations like this before. There was an actual flying sleigh with reindeer pulling it gliding from the back yard to the front. She had no idea how it was suspended in the air like that. There didn't seem to be anything holding it up. From what she could see, it just flew. Levi was in shock. Every time he turned his head he pointed to another thing, his eyes wide and his mouth wide open.

Libby appeared to be overwhelmed with it all. Her long, blonde hair tied up on her head, blue eyes wide, mouth agape, she just stood there taking it all in. It was as if she were standing on the outskirts of Chicago and needed to decide if she were going to plunge right in with the people or just observe everyone else doing so. She stood there, barely noticing her breath freezing in the air as she watched the colors change in front of her very eyes. It didn't matter that it was still somewhat light out. The colors filled the sky.

James saw the beauty in it all. His eyes glistened as the snowflakes landed on his lashes. The grin on his face showed a mixture of childhood excitement and romance. He was amazed at the amount of detail the home owners put in to this Christmas display. It was abundant, over the top, and yet mesmerizing. Each display interacted on some accord with another. James never saw a place be able to blend Christmas themes quite like this place had. Typically, a place with this amount of decorations looked like Christmas throw up. This was nothing of the sort. Angels were interacting with snowmen, who were interacting with elves, the nativity animals went with reindeer who went with Santa Claus. The entire display made sense. It was fascinating to him the amount of thought and creativity that went into this display.

"Their last name is Bronson. It's on the house. Can someone keep them distracted as I try and search through the 'B' in order to find the clue?" Noelle said as soon as she saw the writing on the wall.

"I don't think anyone's paying attention, but if we see someone, we'll get them talking," James replied. He was secretly wondering how on Earth Noelle was going to make it to the house to search the 'B'. She couldn't climb the walls or anything. He found himself slightly amused by the thought of Noelle determined to search. There's no way she was going to figure this one out.

"Thanks!" Noelle said as she took off inconspicuously toward the house.

"What does she think she's going to do?" Libby asked, James in a hushed tone.

"No clue, but it's somewhat entertaining," James replied.

Together, James and Libby watched as Noelle ran really fast and didn't stop when she got to the wall of the house. She made it about three steps up the side of the house and then grabbed the letter 'B' before she came tumbling down and into the bushes. Libby and James stood there in disbelief as they witnessed Noelle go down. "Did you see that? She looked like a ninja going up there like that!" James was in shock but was laughing.

"My goodness! I hope nobody witnessed that!" Libby exclaimed.

"She asked that we keep a lookout for her." Nonchalantly James turned his head around to see if anyone really noticed. Nobody was staring toward the bushes or anything, so he assumed the coast was clear. He gradually made his way toward the bushes, pretending to be an ornament observer like everyone else. Libby did the same. Levi followed suit but was oblivious to what was going on. His eyes were fixed on the flying Santa.

"Noelle, are you okay?" James whispered.

"Yeah, I think so. But I don't see a clue. Do you?" she asked.

"There's not one on the wall where the 'B' was sitting. I'm not seeing one in the bushes, either," James replied. He was still whispering.

"Well that was a waste!" Noelle laughed as she sat herself up, still in the bushes. "Here, grab my hands and help me up."

James helped her and did another quick search of the bushes. Shaking his head when he didn't see anything, he looked at Noelle standing up holding the 'B' behind her back. "How do we suppose we get that back up there?" James asked amused by the whole situation.

"There's a hook on the wall of the house," Noelle explained.

James, grabbing the 'B' walked back into the bushes and jumped trying to put it back where it belonged. After a few tries, he was able to get it up there, but it was a little crooked. "That's going to have to be good enough," he stated.

Noelle looked through the yard at all the decorations and found herself feeling somewhat overwhelmed. "How are we going to find the clue in all this?" she asked.

"Noelle, we found the address, we found the other clues, this is all just Christmas magic. Have faith. I'm sure we'll figure it out."

"We could look at all the decorations that start with a 'B'," Levi suggested shrugging his shoulders.

Libby started searching around the yard. She felt similarly to her sister. There was just so many things in the yard, some with multiple names. Finding a decoration that starts with 'B' could prove to be extremely difficult if not next to impossible. She thought about how many names each thing has as she glanced around. For example, gifts could also be called presents. Happy holidays could be season's greetings. Is Santa in a sleigh or a sled? Is his name Santa or Kris? Are they called sweet rolls or honey buns? Gingerbread boys or gingerbread men? These things make a difference when searching for 'B' words.

After about a half an hour of searching all decorations that they could think of that may start with a 'B', it was dear little Levi to figure it out. "There's a 'B' mommy," he pointed toward the tree.

"Where, Buddy?" Noelle asked, not seeing what it was that he was pointing at.

"It's a 'B'. In the nest. A 'B'."

"What nest? Show me." Noelle was staring near where Levi was pointing. She couldn't for the life of her see anything remotely close to a nest or a 'B'.

Levi grabbed her hand and walked her toward the tree. "Up there. See the bear on the tree? There are bees with it," he pointed.

"He's right!" James exclaimed after realizing what their son was saying. "It's a beehive. There are bees around it," James explained.

"I'm not putting my hand in that thing!"

"Noelle, it's fake. There can't be real bees in the middle of December in Michigan. That doesn't make sense. The beehive goes with the bear. It's a yard ornament."

"That hive looks so real. How do you know the bees aren't hibernating?" she asked.

"I'm with Noelle, that looks too real to me," Libby agreed.

"We don't know, but I mean look at this place," James said as he glanced around. "It's amazing. It wouldn't surprise me in the least if they had a fake beehive that looks real with a clue sitting inside of it. If it makes you feel better, I'll stick my hand in there and find out," James stated.

"No!" Noelle shouted. "That would be ignorant! James, you're deathly allergic to bees."

"I know, that's how sure I am that this is fake."

"I'll do it myself! At least if you're wrong, I won't die from it."

"You could if they're killer bees," Libby informed her.

"We don't have those in Michigan!" Noelle said laughing. Slowly and carefully, Noelle reached up and placed her hand inside the hive. Everyone, including James, was holding their breath. A moment later, Noelle retrieved the clue from the hive.

"You guys were right!" she confirmed. She turned toward Levi and gave him a high-five.

"Let's see what it says," Libby suggested.

"I say we get to the car before we get kicked out of here for destroying the place!" Noelle laughed but was serious at the same time.

James glanced back at his crooked 'B' and agreed. "I'd hate for them to have to call the cops on us for the second time today," he stated.

Libby nodded. Together, as casually as possible, they left the yard and started walking down the street toward their car.

"I'll read it once we're in the car," Noelle said. She was already thinking about what she was going to cook for dinner.

As soon as the car was started, Noelle opened up the little piece of paper that was typed by her mother to reveal their next task.

SINGING A SONG IS FUN TO DO
THAT'S WHY CHRISTMAS CAROLING IS HOW YOU'LL GET YOUR CLUE
IN THE NEIGHBORHOOD SING HIGH AND LOW
FOR THE CLUE THE CORRECT HOUSE YOU MUST GO

"Wow. This one is short and simple," Noelle said.

"It may take forever, but it definitely seems easier. It almost makes me sad," Libby admitted.

"Why's that?" James asked.

"It makes me feel like the game is ending," Libby admitted.

Noelle nodded in agreement. "I wondered the same."

"Well, it's been fun, and we know that it has to end at some point," James reassured them.

In unison, the girls nodded.

"Should we go today or tomorrow?" Libby asked.

"We don't know how many clues we actually have left and it's only four days until Christmas. I say we give it a shot tonight. If we don't end up at the right house, we go caroling again tomorrow. Does that sound okay?" Noelle asked.

"It makes for a long day that's for sure, Levi may want to take a bit of a nap before we eat," James said as he yawned.

"You might need one too!" Noelle laughed.

"Actually, Noelle, I was hoping we would get a chance to talk," James looked at her his eyes pleading.

She knew the time was coming. She agreed.

"How about I make me and Levi some disgusting form of goop for dinner and you and James can go out together and talk and eat. I'll have Levi take a power nap and when you get back, we all go caroling?" Libby asked. "On one condition though."

"What's that?"

"If you guys get into an argument, we're still finishing this up. We've come too far to have it ruined by a disagreement." Libby was serious, and Noelle and James could tell.

"Promise," they both said at the same time.

Libby nodded.

"Um, Libs?"

"Yeah?"

"What kind slop are you feeding my kid?" Noelle bit her lip nervously.

"Probably something like spaghetti from a can."

Noelle cringed. James started to laugh.

"Don't judge me," Libby said. "We can't all be master chefs like you. Besides canned spaghetti is something every kid needs to experience from time-to-time. Be grateful, I am giving your son a normal childhood experience," Libby smiled and gave them a thumbs up.

Noelle took a deep breath and smiled. She wasn't a fanatic about what she gave Levi to eat, she just liked the flavor and health benefits of homemade food. She was sure that Levi's had worse at school. She nodded. "Levi has sandwich stuff in the fridge if he won't eat it."

"What if he loves it?"

"Then that makes you the coolest aunt in the world."

Libby grinned, "I thought you would see it my way!"

Noelle drove all of them back to her house. She reminded Levi to take a quick nap because they were going to go Christmas caroling later on that evening. Levi was excited. He's never been

Christmas caroling before. He agreed to take a nap before he ate dinner. He wasn't sure how he would ever get to sleep though, he was just too excited for going with his family Christmas caroling. In Levi's eyes, he's never had a better Christmas in his entire life.

Chapter Ten
The Conversation and Caroling

"Okay, I'm all ears," Noelle said as she sat across the table from James. They were sitting in a restaurant off in a corner by themselves. The lighting was very dim and compared to the bright snow outside, Noelle had to squint to see him.

"I just feel that we need to discuss the past three years and what had happened..."

"James, it's no big deal. You were gone. I was lonely. I left. I guess I expected you to come chasing after me, but you didn't. You were okay with us leaving."

"Noelle, I was never okay with you leaving. Not once."

"Mmmhmm."

"I'm being serious."

"You never even tried, James," Noelle took a sip of her pop. She could feel her eyes burning and she became grateful for the darkness in the room. She didn't want him to notice her eyes welling up with tears. Though it was likely that he would notice her voice quivering.

"Noelle, listen to me. Please."

Noelle thought about it for a moment. She did promise that he would get an opportunity to speak. She knew she owed him that much after harping on him each time he brought the subject up. But on the flip side, this was her marriage. He owned her heart. She hurt. More than anything she wanted to be with him, wake up next to him, hold him every day. She felt cold, bitter even, to sit in front of him and realize that he hasn't changed. The hurt was so much for her. Her eyes became dry, probably from crying so frequently after she left. Her skin looked older, more blemishes, more wrinkles. She even had to pull a few gray hairs from her head. It drove her crazy to sit across from him and see how time had no effect on him whatsoever.

She felt her emotions turn to a mood. She knew she had to control herself or she would be angry and that had the potential to ruining everything. James was right to do this before Christmas, but it was bittersweet for Noelle, because they had been getting along so well. Here she was sitting in a restaurant of all places watching her fantasy world slip past her again. "I'm listening," she said.

"You asked for my honesty, so I'm giving it to you," James' eyes bore into her. He wanted to articulate his feelings as effectively as possible. He needed to know she heard him. "I was in Tokyo. I was finishing up the project with Dr. Higashi. Every single time I got to a point where I thought we were done, we would have to run the whole system over again to make some detailed changes. We gave him what he asked for and then again, he would have to change his mind. It was like starting from scratch," James took a deep breath. He was hoping he wasn't losing her in the boring details.

"Okay, and?" Noelle asked shortly.

"It was like I couldn't leave. I guess I felt like I was just a hair from being done. I could come back and finally be done with Tokyo altogether. So, I got your letter and I thought to myself, 'she's upset, but she will feel better as soon as this project's done'. To be honest, Noelle, I thought it was going to be a week or two…"

"It was three years, James. What'd you do forget about us?"

"Noelle, in that time I stopped home once."

"So, what if I didn't leave? We would have only seen you one time?"

"No, I made it a point to come home to see you guys. That was it. Trust me, I heard it from everyone. My parents I saw one time in the past three years."

"Why didn't you come after me then?"

"It was a year and a half ago. I came home, reread your letter and stayed with my parents. I couldn't stand to be in the house without you or Levi there."

"And you didn't come to us, why? Oh, right, because you had a new girlfriend by then, right?" Noelle felt her face get hot with anger.

"Noelle, you're not being fair. No, I told you, I didn't date anyone else. Not once."

"Really James?"

"I'm dead serious."

"So when you saw your family why didn't you come for us?"

"I guess I thought it was too late. I tried to call you, but your mother said you were out. My assumption was that you were out with a guy. I didn't want to impose on your happiness."

"What guy?"

"I don't know, Noelle. I just assumed. You're beautiful. I'm sure you're not hurting for dates."

"James, I've been alone this entire time. You don't understand how hard this has been. What was I supposed to tell Levi every night? He used to cry himself to sleep wanting you to be with him at night. He had to start sleeping with me because he missed you so much. I just finally got him in his own bed when he went into first grade."

"I'm sorry."

"No, you're not. You would have come for us."

"I was ashamed. I honestly thought it would be good. That I could be done with it, retire, and make you happy."

"I didn't ask for you to retire James. I asked for your presence."

"I'm here now, Noelle."

"For how long, James? I can't do this to my heart. What about your project? What about Japan? How could you possibly fit me and Levi into your plans."

"Noelle, my plans have always been you and Levi. I just showed them to you the wrong way. I'm truly sorry."

Noelle looked at him and could tell he was being serious. She wanted him to mean it forever, but regardless, she knew he meant it right then.

"Now what?" she asked.

"I guess I was hoping that you would accept my apology."

"I accept your apology. Now what?"

"Noelle, I'm serious."

"Me too, James. I'm serious too. Now what?"

"I want you to continue to be my wife."

"I'm still your wife, we never divorced."

"I'm serious, Noelle."

"I am too, James. I'm still your wife. We never divorced. I'm still on your health insurance plan, you forgot to take me off."

"I didn't forget. In my mind we were always together."

"How is that possible? You haven't held me in three years. James, this is dumb."

"It's possible because I've never fallen out of love with you. I'm being sincere. Noelle, I want you to be my wife."

"What about the houses? You live there. I live here. I have Libby. Levi's in school."

"I could live here too. I will sell the house."

"You would be miserable here."

"I would be ecstatic living on the moon as long as you were there with me."

"That was lame."

"That was truth. I am asking you again, Noelle…" James got down on one knee. "Please forgive me for everything I have ever done wrong to you. Please forgive me for not coming back for you. Please Noelle, forgive me, and I'm begging you to give me another chance as your husband."

Noelle's tears spilled over. They were streaming down her face. This man, the most beautiful man in the world was asking her to be with him. She loved him, she knew she did. This was everything she had ever dreamed of, everything she wanted. But something felt wrong. She didn't want him to be miserable. She knew he liked a bigger house, they were living in a tiny one. She knew there were things he liked that she didn't want him to have to sacrifice. She felt that wasn't fair. It wasn't fair for him to give up on a place he loved to move back with her. She knew she couldn't go back to the state they were living in and leave Libby all alone. It just wasn't right.

"I can't right now, James," she replied.

James squeezed his eyes shut. Casually and slowly he got off of his knee and sat back at the table. His face was pained.

"Look, James, I'm sorry. I just want you to be happy."

"I'm happy when I'm with you."

"I know, but that goes away. You would be miserable in my mom's house. I can't afford another house right now. It's not fair for me to ask you to move here from the home you built there. I have family and friends here."

"Noelle, I have family and friends here too. So what about the house? So what? In the grand scheme of things, that doesn't matter. What matters is us."

"You're right, James. But I don't want you to end up giving up everything to be with me. Your job, your home, your happiness. That is not fair to you," her heart was throbbing with her own words. She tried to be brave, to be credible, but all she really wanted was to say 'yes' and jump into his arms and stay there forever.

"Will you think about it, Noelle?"

"I can't take everything from you. That's not fair to you."

"You already did!" James buried his face in his hands. Taking a deep breath, he pulled his hands through his hair, squeezed his eyes shut, and tried again.

She could see by the blood vessels in his hands that he was tense. She was tense too. "I guess we need to come up with a better solution. I want to be with you, James. But what about your life?"

"Noelle, my life is empty without you and Levi. The rest of the stuff doesn't matter."

"I don't want you to resent me in the future. I don't want you to be one of those guys at a barber shop complaining how your wife ruined your life."

"Noelle, just give me a chance. Will you? I'll tell you what. How about we make a list of everything that we must have in a life. Our hopes, dreams, and the things we just cannot live without. How about we compare those lists and then we can see if we can compromise and make that happen?" James looked hopeful.

Noelle thought that was a fair idea. There were a lot of things that she hoped and dreamed for. There were a few things in life that she needed. One thing she knew she needed was Libby. She couldn't leave her sister after their mom passed away. They were the only family each of them had left. "Okay. I'll make a list."

"Good. I will too. We'll come together in two days and compare our lists. If we can somehow make it work, then we'll stay together. If not, then I promise we can go our separate ways."

"James you act like I want us not to be together. That's not what it is at all. I just don't want you to have to live with a ton of regrets on the account of me."

"Noelle, I'm in love with you. You would give me no regrets."

Noelle bit her lower lip. The truth was, this was the only thing she's been wanting to hear this whole time now. She was afraid. It was hard for her to admit it, but that's exactly what it was. She was scared to death. She didn't want to be responsible for holding James back. She already left him once because of his job. That's not fair to him. She resented Tokyo for that reason.

"I'm in love with you too, James. I just want to be smart."

"I know you do. We'll make a list. You'll see that us being together is the best thing for both of us."

Noelle nodded. She could definitely make a list. She thought about it for a moment. What could she possibly need besides Levi, Libby, and James? In her opinion, that was pretty much the necessities of her list. This task seemed like it could be easy enough. Hopes and dreams was easy too. She had one. One day she wanted to own a restaurant. That was it. Beyond that, she wanted Levi to grow up and be healthy and happy. Noelle thought of one other thing she may want, but she would have to think about it and write it down later. She would give James a list alright, that would not be hard at all.

They ate their food quietly. With only the occasional small talk. Every now and then Noelle would catch James looking at her with a grin. She wanted to ask him what he was smiling at, but she was too busy thinking about the possibilities of the two of them back together again. It seemed like it was rushed, but she thought to herself that the possibility was, it could actually work.

Maybe she would stay in the same city but they could move houses. She wasn't sure though, her mom and dad lived there and she loved that house. She knew if there was a will there was a way. She cursed herself for not saying so. Instead, she would end up writing a list and sharing that with James. The possibility of them being together again, made her stomach flip-flop with joy.

James grinned at her. "What?" She asked, face turning pink from his smile.

"You're beautiful."

"Thank you."

"You know you're going to be my wife again, right?"

"We have to write a list."

"Don't worry, Noelle, it will happen. I have faith."

"I just want the best for everyone."

"It'll happen. In fact, I might as well tell you now, I'm not leaving after Christmas."

"What do you mean?" Noelle couldn't believe her ears. Her heart was racing. She tried to take a bite of food but almost gagged on it. She casually pulled the fork out of her mouth. She couldn't stand the nervousness she was feeling.

"Noelle, I'm not leaving your side. You're my wife and I love you. The list, that's just semantics. Regardless, you're my wife and I'm here. I've made a ton of mistakes, but in my mind, I was doing them for you. I'm not making the same mistakes twice. I'm not leaving after the holidays. I can't handle losing you again."

Noelle bit her bottom lip. She reached her hand across the table and grabbed his. She felt the sparks travel through her arm and down her spine. No matter what happened, she wanted her husband back too. She was just too afraid to tell him that.

"We'll see what happens," she managed. By the time they were done eating, Noelle looked at her plate and only a quarter of her food was gone. She kindly asked for a box, only not to hurt the chef's feelings because she doubted she would even try and eat the food later. The butterflies in her stomach were swarming worse than they did the day of their first kiss. She took a deep breath and wiped her mouth on her napkin. She could hardly believe that James was back in her life and this time with the possibility of staying there forever.

James winked at her, a smile carved onto his face, showing off his jaw. "I love you," he said. He knew what he was doing, and he was doing it well.

"You're trying to torment me on purpose?" she asked.

"Uh-huh," he admitted with a laugh.

"We need to go sing," she said.

James opened his mouth and the chords started to come out. It was their wedding song.

"JAMES! NOT HERE!" Noelle's face was red with both embarrassment and some adoration.

James was cracking up. "I think you're so cute when you're shy!"

Noelle rolled her eyes and pulled him by his arm. "We need to go."

They left the restaurant and when they walked into the doorway they were greeted by Levi. Eyeballing the box of his mother's food, he glanced up at her and Noelle, reading his mind, handed him the box.

"You know this is not natural, right?" Libby stated.

"What isn't?" Noelle asked.

"You have the only kid on the face of the planet that doesn't like canned spaghetti. You shouldn't raise him like that, it's weird."

Noelle laughed. "I told you. He's my son all the way!"

"He's mine too! I'm a sucker for Noelle's cooking!" James said as he smiled, wrapping his arms around her.

"I see you two had your little talk," Libby said.

"We're still trying to figure things out."

"Mmhmm, looks like you got it all figured out to me," Libby said beaming.

"We'll see."

James looked at Libby and winked. "We're back together. I'm not leaving after Christmas."

"I said we'll see!" Noelle shushed him.

Libby nodded and gave James a thumbs up.

When Levi finished, he came out of the kitchen with a grin. "Mom, she tried making me eat slimy, orange spaghetti! It was disgusting!"

"Not normal, Noelle!" Libby shouted from the other room.

Noelle laughed and high-fived her son. "Let's go caroling," she said with a laugh.

Noelle took it upon herself to pull out the clue, just in case they were missing something. She was almost afraid that it was too easy.

SINGING A SONG IS FUN TO DO
THAT'S WHY CHRISTMAS CAROLING IS HOW YOU'LL GET YOUR CLUE
IN THE NEIGHBORHOOD SING HIGH AND LOW
FOR THE CLUE THE CORRECT HOUSE YOU MUST GO

"The only rule I see is that we must stay in this neighborhood and change our octaves, right?" Noelle asked.

"That's what I see too," James agreed.

"Libby, this clue is mostly going to be you. We'll sing as well, but you have the voice."

"Good, this sounds like a lot of fun!" Libby remarked.

After bundling up, they all went outside and looked around. "Do you want to do our old Halloween, trick-or-treating route?" Libby asked.

"That makes the most sense," Noelle replied.

Together, they went to the house to the right of theirs and started to sing. They had no idea if the neighbors were home or not, but they were definitely going to stop at every house to find out, just in case they had the clue they needed.

House to house they went, singing every song they could think of. Libby and James were the best singers and the least shy. For that reason, they sang the loudest. Levi had a higher voice and stood up front, the neighbors just adored him. Noelle tried her best to stay fairly quiet and hide in the back. She didn't like to be the center of attention anyway and she was a terrible singer.

Each house received them differently. Some couples turned on their lights and smiled. Some wouldn't come to the door at all. Some houses invited them in for cookies or tea, while some people had to hold their dogs back and ask them to please leave. None of it seemed to bother them. There was something about going to each house that made it feel even more like Christmas.

One house and elderly lady opened the door. James and Libby started singing 'God Rest Ye Merry Gentlemen' and the old woman stood with her mouth agape, tears pouring down her cheeks. She thanked them ever so much for stopping by. She explained that she was feeling lonely and a little hopeless this Christmas after her husband had to go to a nursing home, but this was the sign telling her that everything was going to be okay. She gave each person a hug and Levi a candy cane. She blessed them and thanked them again for giving her a reason to smile.

Noelle's heart overflowed with emotion. She asked the woman permission if she could come visit her someday. The woman placed her tired, wrinkly hand on her face and said that she would like that very much. Noelle gave her a hug and agreed. James watched how tender and beautiful Noelle could be to a complete stranger and his heart knew beyond a shadow of a doubt that this was the woman he needed to grow old with. He wondered why he ever took her for granted the way he did. Feeling emotional himself, he couldn't imagine how it was possible he lived three years without Noelle. He knew he couldn't do it again. He didn't want to.

House to house, song after song, the family sang together. In the process of their adventure, a few of the neighbors joined them. Most of them commented on how Christmas caroling was something they always saw on TV but was never brave enough to actually go forth and do it. They laughed and sang together, and it was next to impossible not to feel captivated by the true meaning of Christmas.

Noelle, James, Libby, and Levi got so wrapped up in the spreading of holiday cheer that they actually forgot they were on a mission. So much so, that they were surprised when they started to sing at a random blue house down the street, the person handed them a slip of paper after applauding the song. Confused, Noelle looked at it and was shocked to see the clue sitting in her hand. She looked up and smiled and together they sang another song, wishing the home owner a very Merry Christmas.

They finished their mission even though they already had the clue in hand. They were only halfway through their Halloween route and they were determined to finish. All of them agreed that this was one of the highest parts of a Christmas holiday that they ever experienced. The four of them felt magic. The few others that joined them shared in the sentiment.

By the time they made it back to the house, their noses were bright red and cold. Hot chocolate never sounded so good. Noelle decided to take it upon herself to whip up some of her specialty hot chocolate. Libby shook her head as she watched her sister pulling the cocoa, vanilla, and sugar out of the cupboard.

"What?" Noelle asked, confused.

"You are actually making hot chocolate. I didn't even know you could make hot chocolate."

"Well where else do you think hot chocolate comes from?" Noelle asked confused.

"Umm, how about little packets that sit inside a box? That's the only hot chocolate I know."

Noelle shook her head. "Wait till you try this, you'll never want a packet again."

"I'll take your word for it."

"Just wait."

A few minutes later, Noelle brought out four big mugs full of hot chocolate and whipping cream. Libby was impressed when she saw the chocolate syrup drizzled on the top. She raised her eyebrows at Noelle and Noelle shrugged. She knew she goes above and beyond once in a while, but the difference in flavor made it so worth it. Libby took one drink and set the cup on the table. Noelle looked at her and smiled.

"How in the world did you ever figure this out?"

"It's called a recipe."

"I didn't see you pull out a cookbook!"

"I don't need to, I make things all the time, I know the basics of what goes together. But, you could always look at a recipe."

Libby took another sip. "I can't believe this is a thing. It tastes so much better than the packet."

"I told you!"

"You gotta show me how to do that!"

Noelle nodded. "It's actually really simple."

They sat together in silence, all of them warming up with the help of hot chocolate. The hot cup felt great on Noelle's hands. Every now and then she would place the cup up against her cheek. She wanted to place it against her ear, but she was afraid that she would get her hair in it and then her hair would be all sticky and gross. She closed her eyes and felt the heat against her mouth as she lingered in the moment. At that moment, Noelle felt to be the luckiest woman on earth. If she were to open her eyes, the man of her dreams would be sitting next to her hoping to be reunited with her. She hadn't felt this giddy since their wedding day. If she were to look onto her other side, her beautiful little boy, a perfect combination of her and James' love for each other was sitting there embracing his holiday, with both of his parents. Directly in front of her was her sister, her closest female friend, whom she was grateful she had a lifetime of shared experiences with. Noelle felt truly blessed.

"Hey, you got the clue, didn't you?" Libby asked, remembering the purpose for their experience.

"Yes, it's right here." Noelle pulled the clue out and sat it on the table.

> **THIS CLUE MAY MAKE YOU MINGLE**
> **I WANT YOU TO GO SEARCHING FOR KRIS KRINGLE**
> **ALL OVER I KNOW HE IS**
> **TOO BAD SO MANY ARE IN THIS BIZ**
> **SING JINGLE BELLS TO EACH ONE**
> **UNTIL ONE GIVES YOU A GIFT OH WHAT FUN**
> **THE GIFT IS HEAVY BUT ITS YOUR NEXT CLUE**
> **HOPEFULLY BY SEEING IT YOU CAN FIGURE OUT WHAT TO DO**

"I had a hunch that the last clue was too easy. Your mom was just giving us a break for this one," James said. "Do you know how many Santas are around just a couple of days before Christmas?"

"Are they counting the bell ringers too?" Noelle asked.

"She's counting every single one of them. This clue in itself could take days," Libby replied. "Even at the hospital we have random Santas."

"Does it make a difference that she said, 'Kris Kringle' instead of Santa?" Noelle asked.

"Maybe? Hopefully. I'd say we do those first," Libby stated.

"How can you distinguish the difference between Santa Claus and Kris Kringle?" James asked.

"I guess we go to the most famous places first and then look at their name tag. Maybe we can check the local paper?" Noelle suggested.

"We have to sing again, my voice is going to be hoarse," Libby complained.

"Come on guys, it'll be fun!" Levi announced above everyone's talking.

Everyone turned to look at Levi. He was right. Again, the four of them together. Singing Jingle Bells to random Santas. Honestly, it was going to be fun, even if it did take a little while. They were already forgetting to appreciate the togetherness, the moment, their mother's last project for them. Noelle reached over and scratched her son's head. He was such a good person to keep them all in perspective. She was proud of herself for raising such a bright young man.

All of them were exhausted after such a long day of searching for clues. Three hours caroling in the evening, and the entire morning was spent searching for the street that was fun and then invading the person's property by trespassing. It had been a long but wonderful day. They were all too tired to sleep on the floor. Levi and James slept in Levi's bed that night. Libby took the couch. She thought it would be too weird to sleep in her mother's bed. Noelle slept by herself in her bed. She had offered Levi to crash with her, so James would have more room, but Levi and James both were okay bunking together.

Noelle made sure the front door was locked and then went into the bedroom to tuck her son in. James was in the bathroom brushing his teeth. She fixed Levi's blankets and kissed him goodnight.

"Mom, is Daddy going to stay with us, now?" Levi asked.

"I'm not sure, Buddy. Why do you ask?"

"I want him to stay with us. I love him big."

"He loves you big, too." Noelle bent over her son and kissed him on the forehead.

"Daddy loves you big too."

"We'll see." Noelle said feeling her face flush.

"He told me he does. Don't tell Daddy, but I love you the biggest!"

"Well, I love you the biggest, most hugest, gigantic-est of them all!" Noelle said.

"Goodnight mom."

"Goodnight son."

Noelle left the room, shutting the light off as she left. She was startled because James was standing in the doorway. "I didn't see you," she said.

"I love you the biggest," James said as he gently pulled her close to him.

Noelle held him tight. Her face nestled in his neck. She immediately found the beat of his heart and she absorbed the sound as if it were the last thing she would ever hear. She inhaled deeply, taking James in. She wondered if he could possibly love her bigger than she loved him. She highly doubted it.

Chapter Eleven
The Search for Kris Kringle

With all the excitement from the night before, Noelle overslept. It was the first time she slept late in what felt like years. She woke up to the smell of bacon cooking. At first, she thought the house was on fire and she jumped out of bed to go see what was going on. Then the smell hit her, and she started to laugh. She wondered who was cooking.

She came around the corner to see Levi sitting on Libby's lap reading a book together. Their empty plates were sitting on the table next to them. James was wearing Noelle's number one chef apron and was flipping some eggs. Noelle flinched as she watched him struggle with not breaking the yolk as he scraped the bottom of the pan with the spatula. It made her smile, actually flipping the eggs in the pan is a lot simpler, but she would never burst his bubble like that.

"Smells good," she said.

"It's not nearly as good as yours, but I figured we have a long day ahead of us and you were sound asleep, so I took it upon myself to make sure we all ate before we left. I hope you don't mind."

"No, it's actually kind of nice to wake up to a hot breakfast."

James handed her the plate. Noelle grinned at the smiley face he made her out of the bacon and eggs. The bacon was a little overdone, but it was definitely edible. Noelle took a bite with some of her toast and was overcome with gratitude for her family and how they look out for each other. She knew that the day ahead was going to be difficult, but she also knew they could and would make the best out of it and enjoy time together.

"So, we're on a mission to find Kris Kringle," she said as she wiped her face off on a paper towel.

"I don't even know where to start," Libby chimed in.

"I think that's the point. Let's just start. I don't think it's that weird, we find every Santa we can find and sing Jingle Bells to each one. If they give us a gift, we know," Noelle reassured her.

"The gift has to be heavy. It's not going to be like a candy cane or anything," James added.

"Right. We've got this!" Noelle smiled at her family.

James wiped his hands dry as he nodded his head. They geared up to go outside and start their day. First thing's first, they decided to try the mall. This close to Christmas, there's always a Santa at the mall. What they didn't think to take into consideration as they were starting their day was that this close to Christmas the lines for Santa would be exceptionally long. They could end up spending most of their day in lines and not even find the right guy. The rules stated they had to stay together. So, they hoped for the best as they went on their adventure.

They made it to the mall just moments after the mall opened. The first item on their list was to find Santa. They were hoping because they were there so early, they would be able to beat the traffic. Fortunately, they were right. Santa only had one child in line and one on his lap when they made it over to him. The child on his lap had to have been about two-years-old and was screaming. His voice could be heard throughout the stores in the surrounding areas. Mom was doing everything she could to get a nice picture with the baby. Santa's helpers who were dressed as elves were singing and dancing and peek-a-booing trying to get the child to laugh. Nothing was working.

James walked up to one of the elves and pulled her hat off and pointed toward the lady's head. At first the lady was appalled, but then the toddler started to laugh. James dropped the hat back onto the elf and pulled it off again. This time the toddler was in hysterics. The elf whispered 'thank you' to James and he did this a few more times, while the photographer was taking pictures.

When they were all said and done, the mom walked over to James and gave him a big hug. She thanked him and told him how good with children he was. That was all good and fine until Noelle heard her say that she wished she had a guy in her life that was good with kids like James was. She went on to discuss how her guy left her. James smiled and nodded. He added the appropriate condolences and shrugged a few times while the woman was giving him her story. Noelle's green eyes turned 12 shades greener during this interaction. She didn't like it one bit.

The woman handed James a business card and thanked him again. James shoved the card into his pocket absentmindedly and rejoined the line to visit with Santa. Libby smiled at him and told him how good with kids he was and then she slyly added that he was good with women too. James laughed and shrugged, humbly shaking his head. Noelle thought to herself how her sister is a traitor and she found herself feeling downcast. She ruffled her son's hair and didn't say a word to anyone.

It was finally their turn to see Santa. They walked up to him, Levi taking a spot on his lap without any hesitation at all, and together the four sang Jingle Bells. Santa smiled and started talking to Levi about what he wanted for Christmas. Levi described the bike he wanted in full detail. Noelle looked down toward her feet, sad that she couldn't afford him that bike, but hopeful he would like the scooter as consolation prize. A few moments later, they were given a candy cane and a picture of all of them with Santa.

Seeing the picture Noelle found herself feeling even more frustrated. She compared herself to the single mom that James was talking to and realized she must be ten years her senior. Noelle was in her thirties, the girl had to be in her twenties. Noelle saw the hints of wrinkles forming around her eyes. That woman was full of zest and makeup. Noelle looked at James and it didn't matter that he was her age, James was gorgeous. Older men are more sophisticated to younger women and they age beautifully. Women seem to become old hags according to the fashion world and Noelle was feeling just that. Though to be honest, she never really felt that way before, but seeing James interacting with that woman and how she was flirting with him, made Noelle feel far more archaic than usual.

Libby reported that she had to use the bathroom. James took that as his opportunity to announce that he would be back in just a few minutes, leaving Noelle and Levi sitting alone on a bench in the center of the mall. Levi was going on and on about how he wanted a bike and Noelle felt flushed. She even considered possibly taking the scooter back to the store to buy him the bike. She didn't like that idea because she wanted to be smart financially and make solid decisions, but on the other hand, Levi has never showed such a desire to have anything like that before. A day that seemed to start out so well for Noelle was quickly becoming a bust.

"You wanna talk about it?" Libby asked startling Noelle out of her thoughts.

"Not really."

"You know he's head over heels for you, right? He didn't think twice about that girl. In fact, just the opposite actually. You should have seen the look he gave me when she was rattling on and on about things. He gave me a plea for help."

"It's not just that."

"You're feeling old because you only have a good 5-8 years left to have more children?"

"What?! No! But thanks for that!"

"Then what is it?"

Noelle leaned into her sisters' ear and said something about the bike.

"Have James get it, you know he can afford it."

"That's the point, Libby, I don't want to have to depend on him. What if things don't work out?"

"Then don't get it. Frankly, I think he could care less, especially considering what you did get him."

"I hope you're right, but I feel really bad about it."

"You really need to stop worrying so much. That's what's causing all those wrinkles!"

"Libby! That doesn't help at all."

"I'm just messing with you. Chill out. Everything is great. Relax. You'll get more worry lines."

"Libby!"

Libby started to laugh.

"What's so funny?" James asked, startling them both.

"Oh, Noelle's jealous of a girl ten years younger than her and she thinks she's antique and wrinkly. She wants more kids but her biological clock is ticking and so she's feeling insecure. In addition to that, she has a problem with anxiety and she's showing lines of worry all over her face. If you look close enough you can see a crow's landing spot right there near her eye. Oh, and she's financially strapped so she thinks that could likely ruin Christmas."

Noelle's face turned purple. Leave it to her sister to take things to a whole different level of humiliating.

"See how silly all that sounded?" Libby made her point raising an eyebrow toward Noelle.

"Noelle, if you need help for things, I told you I would help," James reminded her.

"Trust me, I'm fine," Noelle said. She was frustrated. She didn't want his help. She wanted him to be there, but she couldn't tell him that either. Additionally, she couldn't help but wonder why he didn't deny anything about the woman or Noelle's aging. She knew she was just jumping to conclusions, but it would have been nice to hear him say something. She took a deep breath and forced a smile. "We have more Kris Kringles' to find."

They went through every store in the mall, just in case there was a Santa anywhere else. Not really having any luck, aside from a skinny kid wearing a Santa hat in the mall's drug store, which they took it upon themselves to sing Jingle Bells to him too, they didn't see another. Once they cleared the mall and purchased a huge pretzel with cheese sauce for everyone, they decided to look at other locations that may have a Santa. James picked up a leftover newspaper to see if he saw any advertised. The only one they saw was one for pets at a pet store. Since the pet store was across the street, they decided to give that one a try while they searched for more.

At the pet store, Noelle was dumbfounded at how many people were there to get pictures with their pets and Santa. Noelle thought that there were likely more pets getting pictures taken than there were children. It was so strange to her. The cats and dogs were dressed in anything from fur coats and sweaters, to golf caps and diamond studded collars. She felt funny realizing she didn't even dress her son as classy as some of the animals looked. She took a glimpse of their picture with Santa and laughed. This was a totally different situation altogether.

By the time it was their turn, Santa almost seemed confused that they didn't have an animal with them. The group sang Jingle Bells and Santa laughed, stating that he only had a cat treat or dog biscuit to give to them. They just shrugged taking the dog biscuit and putting it with their candy canes from earlier. James bought the photo and also while he was there got a bag to put the things in. He figured he might as well start collecting the photos and later scrapbook them as a Christmas to always remember. If they were lucky, Levi would collect enough candy canes through this journey that he could just put them on the Christmas tree. It would make for a decent variety.

    Not seeing anything else in the paper, they decided to ask around to see if people know where a Santa may be lurking. It wasn't a popular question and it did tend to take people off guard, however, after asking a few people they were able to come up with two more locations for a Santa Claus. One was at the toy store down the street and around the corner. The other was clear across town at a grocery store. They decided the toy store was first. In typical Libby style, she grabbed her notebook and started to make a list. She had so many lists made from these clues that she started to feel like good ol' St. Nick herself.

    The toy store was a zoo. Not in the fashion where they found their last Santa which was actually filled with animals, but in the sense that there were toys and kids everywhere! It was actually overwhelming to everyone, including Levi. They learned that Santa was sitting in a corner on the far side of the store. Because of the chaos in the store, they didn't pay too much attention to whether or not there was a line that they were cutting in front of or if there wasn't. They just wanted to get the task done with and leave. They walked up to the Santa Claus, which by the way was beautiful. This Santa had to have been the best looking, most realistic Santa out of them all so far, and they shook his hand and sang the song. Santa smiled at them and handed each of them a coloring book and crayons, along with a candy cane. The lady who none of them noticed was there, gave them a polaroid picture of them. They thanked everyone and left the store as fast as possible.

"You don't think this is the clue by chance, do you?" Libby asked with hope plastered to her face.

James shook his head. "It said it'd be heavy, didn't it?"

Noelle nodded. She still wasn't very talkative, especially considering that James seemed to be a single mom magnet. She couldn't help but pay attention after the first incident in the mall. At the toy store she saw how women would turn their heads and stare at him. She half considered asking him to put his ring back on just for that reason alone, but she decided that would be ridiculous. Though she was kind of mad at herself because he did ask her to be with him again, and her crazy self, refused to give him a sold straight answer. Regardless, she now regretted that decision as she was observing women's reaction to her guy. She reached into her purse and pulled out the clue and handed it to him.

**THIS CLUE MAY MAKE YOU MINGLE
I WANT YOU TO GO SEARCHING FOR KRIS KRINGLE
ALL OVER I KNOW HE IS
TOO BAD SO MANY ARE IN THIS BIZ
SING JINGLE BELLS TO EACH ONE
UNTIL ONE GIVES YOU A GIFT OH WHAT FUN
THE GIFT IS HEAVY BUT ITS YOUR NEXT CLUE
HOPEFULLY BY SEEING IT YOU CAN FIGURE OUT WHAT TO DO**

"This clue is going to be different from the rest," James stated after studying the clue for a moment.

"I think so too," Libby agreed. "Just the way she said, hopefully we can figure out what to do."

"Will we know it when we see it?" Noelle asked.

"All we know is that it's heavy," James stated.

"And she called it a gift," Libby added.

"Let's keep looking for it," Levi, always the trooper, suggested.

The rest of them nodded. Not wanting to ask in the vicinity of the toy store, due to the crowds, they just decided to drive across town and see about the one at the grocery store. They decided they would talk to more people on that side of town to see if there were any more Santa's. In the meanwhile, while they were driving, they kept their eyes out and ears on the radio to see if they could learn where more may be.

They walked into the grocery store and started walking up and down the aisles looking for Santa. Finding him, perched up near the produce section, Levi ran to him and jumped up on his lap. This Santa was African American. His white beard was crisp and real. He had gentle eyes and a jolly smile. This Santa was Levi's favorite so far. After a few minutes of conversation, the four sang the song to him. Smiling, the Santa handed them a few candy canes and a homemade gingerbread house kit. They thanked him kindly and left the store.

"This is getting to be irritating," Libby sighed.

"Do you think it isn't Santa? Do you think if we checked the phone book there may be some Kris Kringle's in there?" Noelle asked, coming to the realization that just maybe their mother tricked them again.

"Anything is worth a try at this point," Libby stated.

"We can try that, but didn't the clue say there would be a lot of them? She said something about there's many in this biz. I'm assuming in the Santa biz. But, she could be throwing us for a loop too," James stated.

"Well, it doesn't hurt to check the phone book. If that doesn't work, we keep searching Santa's," Noelle stated.

"We can't sing to them over the phone. Let's get some addresses and we'll go Jingle Bells caroling at the address. That may work," Libby said.

They drove home for lunch and to find a phone book. They each ate a salad as Noelle went searching through the K's. She forgot how much she relied on her computer and internet when it came to making searches, finding maps, and things like that. Actually, flipping pages of an old phonebook felt strange. What was even stranger is that she was lucky to find this phonebook, she wasn't even sure if they made them anymore.

There were four Kris Kringle's in the phone book. Feeling a little uneasy, Noelle checked the addresses and decided to try the two that were closest to home first. She was grateful she wasn't going to have to go alone. It felt a little strange to be seeking out people to go sing to. Christmas caroling was one thing, but actually looking in the phonebook to seek the recipients of the song, seemed just a little over the top. As she gave Libby the addresses, she took a deep breath of her mother's candle and silently asked her mom for some guidance regarding this clue. Feeling a little more calm, it was time to go.

They drove to the closest house first. They walked up toward the gate and as soon as they tried to open it, out of nowhere a dog came bearing teeth. Noelle jumped back. Libby, trying to be brave, started to speak to the dog as if it were a small child. The dog, a German Shepherd who was much smarter than Libby had given consideration, looked at her like she was crazy. It stood there watching as Libby tried again at the gate. The dog shook its head and immediately jumped bearing all teeth. Libby jumped back and shook her head.

"This isn't going to work. Let's try the next house, we can always come back to this one later," she said.

Noelle and James agreed. Levi was already half way to the car. He wasn't taking any chances with a growling dog. Back into the car, Libby's phone went off. She smiled and then turned the ringer off.

"Who was that?" Noelle asked curiously.

"That was just Nate," Libby replied.

"Nate?"

"The guy from the other night."

"Why are you avoiding him?" Noelle asked confused.

"He was too good to be true. I liked him and I don't want to be disappointed," Libby answered matter-of-factly.

"Libs, you need to give the guy a chance. Especially if you liked him."

"What if he comes out to be a player or something like that?"

"What if he is Mr. Right?" Noelle argued.

James laughed. "Women make no sense sometimes."

"You should at least text him back. Maybe he knows of some Kris Kringles that we don't," Noelle suggested.

Libby shrugged. "I guess, but what if he wants to talk to me? Then what? Or what if he wants to meet up with me? How could I get out of that?" she asked.

"Libs, maybe you should meet up with him then. We're here, nothing's going to happen to you."

Libby bit her lower lip.

"Libby you're scared. All this time you laugh at me for my insecurities, and here you are doing the same thing. What advice would you give to me? You would say, Noelle just give him a chance. So, Libby, just give him a chance," Noelle was pointing at her sister.

Libby grinned sheepishly. "Fine!"

A few minutes later, Libby announced to the car that Nate knew of a Santa at the place where the ball was.

"Well we're closer to there than we are the next Kris Kringle's house. Should we try that first?" Noelle asked.

James nodded. "That makes sense since we're right there."

Noelle parallel parked her car. She couldn't help but admire how well this place was decorated. It made the whole street look elegant. Together they walked in to go find Santa Claus. Under the same mistletoe that introduced Libby and Nate, James kissed Noelle softly. Libby avoided the mistletoe at all cost. Walking through the hallway, they immediately saw the display.

"The house of Kris Kringle," Noelle pointed out.

It was a gingerbread house styled layout. There was a huge throne that Santa was sitting on. Instead of the traditional red and white suit, he was wearing green. He had the long beard, again very real, but looked more like the older country styled Santa. Sitting next to him appropriately was a plate of cookies. Noelle felt a sense of childhood excitement as she stood in line. The red carpet was lined with nutcracker soldiers. The area still had the silver and white snowflakes and the massive Christmas tree. The whole thing went together superbly.

"Libby, I was hoping I'd see you here."

Libby turned around, her cheeks pinkening, as she saw Nate approaching her. He was wearing some gray slacks and a sweater vest over his dress shirt. His brown dress shoes tied the outfit together perfectly.

"You were?" she asked, feeling the butterflies tickling her tummy.

"Of course I was," he replied.

Libby blushed. Noelle rolled her eyes. The truth was, she loved getting that type of attention from James, but she was still a hair jealous from earlier that day. She never realized how brave women were when it came to expressing their attraction for men. She wasn't like that.

Nate asked Libby what she was doing looking for Kris Kringle, anyway. Libby explained to him that it was a part of the clue game. They had to sing Jingle Bells and then see if he gives them a present or not. The gift is the next clue.

"Okay, Libby, aside from finding and solving clues, which I guess makes you like a private investigator, what other things do you do?"

"I'm currently a nurse practitioner, but I'm in med school to become a doctor," Libby replied.

"A nurse? Where?" Nate asked. He was laughing, and Libby couldn't figure out what he was laughing at.

"At General Hospital. I'm an emergency room nurse," she explained.

Nate shook his head.

Libby gave him a funny look.

"I'm sorry, Libby. I don't mean to laugh. It's just that, I'm a physician," Nate said.

"Where?"

"General."

"Why is it that I don't know you, then?"

"I'm new to the area. I just moved from Ann Arbor to here, for this position."

"Well, I hope that you enjoy our town," Libby said reaching for her words not really sure what else to say.

"I would enjoy it more if I had someone I could take out and perhaps show me the area," Nate grinned at her. He then leaned in and gently brushed her on the cheek.

Noelle's face was on fire. The man was gorgeous, smart, and a working professional. She wondered if he was into some of the same things she enjoyed too, such as the occasional mountain climb, cross country biking, white water rafting, or perhaps trying new things like sky-diving.

It was their turn to visit Kris Kringle. Levi propped himself onto Santa's lap. Levi looked at Santa and smiled. When asked what he wanted for Christmas, unlike with the other Santa's Levi leaned in to Santa's ear and told him a secret. Santa started to laugh.

"Levi, that is a tough, tough thing to make happen." Santa glanced at James and Noelle and smiled. Then Santa leaned in to Levi and said, "Even if your mom and dad don't stay together, I do know that both of your parents love you very, very much. I can see it on their faces!"

Levi gave Santa a thumbs up. "I could also use a puppy," Levi said smiling. He leaned in and whispered to Santa, "they think I want a bike."

Santa winked at Levi. "Your dad staying around, puppy, bike, nothing too big, right Levi?" Santa laughed.

Levi laughed too. "I told you it was a lot!"

"I have a feeling you'll be pleasantly surprised this year, son," Santa said.

Without further ado, Levi went right into song. Noelle catching on also started to sing. Noelle, shook her head and smiled. She looked at Nate and whispered, "I need to save them," and she began to sing too. It was James to join last.

Santa grinned and reached down toward his bag of candy. He pulled up a paper bag and handed it to Levi. "Be careful, kiddo, this bag is heavy."

Levi smiled. "I am looking forward to seeing you, Santa."

Santa placed his finger beside his nose and gave Levi a nod. He then winked at him and Levi jumped off his lap and looked at his mom.

"Here's the clue, Mom," he said as he handed her the bag. He never had to look in it to know.

"Libby, your voice is amazing!" Nate said, as he and Libby walked toward the door.

"Yeah, I'm only a part time nurse, I sing most weekends," Libby smiled. She wasn't the type of woman to get stage fright or anything of the sort, but she was definitely humble. She was never the type of person to brag or feel like she was better than others.

"Is there anything you can't do?" Nate asked.

"Yup, I can't cook. In fact, yesterday I tried to feed my nephew canned spaghetti. He wouldn't touch it no matter how hard I tried. One bite and the kid almost threw up," she laughed.

"Good to know. I grill once in a while, but I'm not much of a cook myself," Nate admitted.

"See, so we're not soulmates," Libby teased.

"Or we go out every night of the week," Nate replied.

"I'd be starving if it wasn't for my sister," Libby admitted. "She's the best cook I know. She's going to open a restaurant one day," Libby stated.

"We'll see about that."

"You will. Trust me, I'll fund it myself," Libby laughed.

"She's that good, huh?" Nate asked.

Noelle took this as her opportunity. "How about you come for dinner one of these days and find out? You're somewhat new to the area, do you have plans for Christmas?" Noelle offered.

Libby shot her a look. Nate noticed it and smiled.

"Actually, I don't have plans. My family is in Wisconsin and I've been here for about eight months, but between work, sleep, and trying to find a better apartment, I haven't made many friends. I would be honored to come. Besides home cooked food sounds wonderful. That is, if Libby doesn't mind."

Everyone looked at Libby. She was blushing. She was so used to being alone that she felt awkward inviting a guest. "Sure, you can come."

Noelle grinned her *evil sister* grin. "So, Nate, is there anything you're allergic to, won't eat, or absolutely love?"

"No, no, and anything. I'm pretty easy going," Nate replied.

James had to take a phone call, so he excused himself for a moment. Noelle smiled and nodded and continued talking to Nate. Levi was dancing around the hall singing along to the Christmas music. Libby, brushing her long blonde hair out of her face, seemed to be far more uptight than usual. Noelle could tell that she really liked this guy. Noelle also knew that her sister was going to intentionally try and blow it. She pulls away from relationships for some unapparent reason. She always claims that the guy just isn't right. Noelle was waiting for that tagline this time too, however, Libby didn't say that yet. Instead she keeps saying, 'he seems too good to be true.'

Noelle watched as Libby and Nate went off on a different conversation, something regarding hiking or horseback riding. Noelle wasn't paying too close attention because she wanted to see what the clue was that Levi handed her. Opening the bag, Noelle's hand trembled as she pulled out a snow globe. She looked at it closely and tried to figure out the clue. Inside the globe was a building in between two pine trees, inside the door of the building was a lit fireplace. The building looked vaguely familiar, but Noelle couldn't place it.

Noelle tipped the snow globe over to see if the bottom said anything. It was blank. There was a key on the bottom to wind it up. Noelle wound it and listened carefully. The song was one that she immediately recognized. It was her mom and dad's wedding song. Noelle wondered what her mother was trying to do. Her eyes teared up and Noelle told Libby she was going to go outside and catch some fresh air for a moment, to please watch Levi until James came back. Libby agreed.

On her way outside, the door man stopped her. Noelle gave him a curious look and the guy pointed up toward the mistletoe. Noelle stood there and waited. In just a moment's time, a guy with his daughter came through the door. Noelle smiled at him. She quickly glanced behind him to see if a wife was coming. When she didn't notice one, she bit her lower lip nervously and asked him if he could help her out.

Smiling, the man agreed. He carefully, leaned in and gently rested his palm against Noelle's cheek and gave her a soft peck on the lips. 'Thank you', she mouthed to him. He winked at her and nodded, mouthing toward her, 'any time.' He let go of her cheek and walked in to go see Santa Claus. Noelle glanced at the doorman as if to prove a point, he nodded, and she walked outside.

James saw the entire transaction and for the first time since him coming back to Michigan, he felt engulfed in pain. His heart felt like it broke into a million pieces. It was simple, just a kiss, but to watch how eager the guy was to help his wife out, to watch Noelle thank him like that, his insides burned. Not wanting to jump to conclusions and miscommunication that tends to always show up on the movies, James decided to approach Noelle, frankly, with how he was feeling.

He didn't expect to see her reacting in the way she was. As James approached, Noelle was leaning against the car, sobbing.

"Noelle, what's the matter?" He asked, feeling a little guilty for being upset moments before.

"Nothing," she said, coolly.

"Noelle, talk to me. We need to talk," James was adamant.

Noelle heard something different in his voice. She turned toward him, to face him. She could tell something was bothering him, but she wasn't sure what it was. Not worrying too much about it, she handed him the snow globe.

"What's this?" he asked.

"This is the clue."

"What is it?" He was confused, staring at the globe.

"Wind it up," she said.

James obeyed. He let go of the key and listened. He recognized the tune from a long time ago. It was a song from sometime in the late 70's. "Isn't this the song that we played for your mom at our wedding?" James asked.

"Yes, that's my parent's wedding song," Noelle informed him.

"Yeah. I remember," James recalled after listening to it again. The two fell silent as they listened to the snow globe that her mother gave them.

When the song stopped neither one of them said anything. They just stood there, looking at the snow globe as if trying to read it like a crystal ball. It didn't do anything. It was just the building between the trees with the fireplace on in the building.

It was Noelle to break the silence. "I feel like we've come so far but I don't get this one at all," she admitted.

"Mmmhmm," he agreed.

"What's wrong? You seem off," Noelle asked him.

"I watched you kiss that guy," James admitted.

"Oh, under the mistletoe?" Noelle laughed.

"He was into it."

"No, he wasn't. I asked him to do me a favor because the doorman wouldn't let me leave."

"You could have waited for me."

"I didn't know how long you were going to be. You disappeared with your phone. Which by the way, that's getting pretty secretive too," Noelle pointed out.

James couldn't deny it because he knew it was true. "I just hated walking in on that. You're the love of my life, Noelle. The last thing I wanted to see was you kissing another guy."

"Oh, it must have been just as comforting as watching that woman hug you and give you her contact information," Noelle contested.

James nodded. "She didn't kiss me."

"What do you want from me?" Noelle asked.

"I want you and I to be a family again."

"Did you write your list?"

"Not yet, but I will."

"Like I said, we'll talk about it then. Who were you on the phone with?" Noelle asked, knowing that he wouldn't tell her but wanting to prove a point that their relationship isn't what it once was.

"That's not fair, Noelle."

"James, we'll talk about it then. And if you get jealous of guys kissing me under the mistletoe, maybe you shouldn't be sneaking off on the phone in places that contain a ton of mistletoe," she was matter-of-fact, but she wasn't angry.

"Noelle, come here."

She looked at him, her heart racing. He closed his eyes and gently gave her a kiss. Placing his forehead against hers, he rubbed his nose with hers and then smiled. "I had to make sure his lips weren't the last lips on you," he stated.

"James, come here," she whispered with a smile tugging at her lips.

James, who was already leaning against her raised his eyebrows. "Hmm?" he asked.

Quietly grabbing snow and carefully putting it down his neck as she went in for a hug, James started to scream. Noelle laughed and began to run, carefully keeping the snow globe close to her.

"You're going to pay for that Noelle!" he said chasing her. James quickly grabbed some snow and ran toward her with a huge pile in his hands.

Noelle ducked and continued to run as he went in after her. She ran past the doorman but she couldn't get past the mistletoe. The second doorman stood in front of her and told her she needed to stay due to tradition. Noelle stood under the mistletoe and waited for James to rescue her. Instead, the guy that kissed her earlier came to her aid. As he went in for his second round with Noelle, James cut in.

"Um, not so fast, buddy. This is my wife," James scooped her in his arms and kissed her passionately under the mistletoe.

Noelle could hear a few whistles and screams in the background. With a red face, she came up and grinned. That's when she took the snow to her head. "Got you!" James said through his laughter. With snow melting down her face, Noelle couldn't have been happier. All of her insecurities from earlier in the day had left her. She felt like a whole new person, one whose life was totally complete.

Chapter Twelve
The Unwritten Clue

Noelle sat on her bed, turning the snow globe over in her hands. For the life of her she couldn't figure out what her mother was wanting them to figure out regarding this clue. There were no words, no anything. It was just that, a building in between two pine trees and a fireplace on the inside. Not to leave out her parents' wedding song. *What does this mean?* She wondered to herself.

She sat the globe down on the dresser and went to bed. With Christmas being two days away, she didn't even have time to bake cookies yet. She had been able to sneak upstairs to finish Libby's gift. She just worked on it piece by piece, little by little. She was grateful to have that done. If it weren't for James' help, she wouldn't have. There's been a few nights he was able to keep her occupied while she pretended to be wrapping gifts for Levi, or being too tired to visit. The truth was, James wrapped all Levi's presents while Noelle was keeping everyone busy. She had to admit they had a good system going.

Dressed in her pajamas and bathrobe, Noelle went to the kitchen to get a glass of water before she turned in for the night. She wasn't expecting to see Libby sitting by herself at the table.

"What's wrong?" Noelle asked, sensing a little negativity in the air.

"Nothing really. I'm just thinking," Libby lied.

"I know you better than that. Really what's going on?"

Libby looked at her sister. She had tears in her eyes and Noelle was surprised. She hasn't seen her sister cry in years. She didn't even cry at their mom's memorial service. Crying was never

Libby's style. She was more of the fight for what's right type of woman. Libby bit her bottom lip and shook her head.

"I don't know," she almost whispered.

"What do you mean? Is it Christmas? Mom? Life in general? Work? Libby, what's going on?"

"I think I just feel... stressed... different maybe. I'm not really sure. This is our first Christmas without mom, but the truth is, I've been having a great time. It's been one of my best Christmases actually. I know that sounds awful, but it has, and I think that makes me feel bad. Then, there's Nate. He's like perfect. Seriously, perfect. You know he's a doctor, right? How hot is that? He's a really great looking doctor..."

"Okay? So why is this a problem?" Noelle was smiling. She knew exactly what was wrong with her sister. Libby was feeling guilty for her happiness and was trying to sabotage it. Libby was a pro at escaping great things.

"I don't know. Do you know how many women like doctors? If they didn't those TV shows wouldn't be so popular."

"You're jealous?"

"No, I'm just not stupid. Doctors aren't the faithful type."

"So, enjoy it while it lasts?" Noelle watched her sister closely. She knew Libby never really cared too much about competition with other women. Libby was confident, fun, she wasn't the raging jealous type.

"What if I'm alone for the rest of my life?" That's when the tears started to flow.

Noelle looked at her sister and realized, not only was she happy, she was also afraid. With Mom gone and Noelle talking to James again, Libby was afraid of being left totally by herself. It wasn't the man she was worried about, though Noelle had a hunch she was falling hard for Nate, it was the fear of not having anyone around. "You know I'm not going anywhere, right? I already told James that."

"I know. But I don't want you stuck here because of me. I don't want to hold you back, Noelle."

"You're not. I love it here. Levi loves it here. I'm staying because I want to."

"Really?"

"Really."

Libby wiped her eyes. "Thank you."

"You're welcome, but I must tell you, you're a fool if you don't date Nate. Imagine the whole nursing station will be sickly jealous of you."

"Are you kidding me? They already are! I don't need that type of problem! I have enough explaining how my face doesn't wrinkle. I swear they think I'm a vampire as it is!" Libby laughed at her own joke.

"Seriously, though. Nate seems to be a good guy. Give him a chance."

"We'll see. I don't want to turn into the jealous type. Have you seen how beautiful he is? My goodness, I'm afraid the med unit would lose their minds if I dated him. I can't imagine the backlash. They already go out of their way to try and find mistakes I've made. I'm telling you, being kind of pretty and working in medicine is not easy! It's sad how people want people to fail so badly. I'm not even a mean person. If I were, I'd be really in for it."

Noelle understood exactly what her sister was saying. Unfortunately, that was a problem Libby has had for years. People genuinely didn't like her because of how she looked and how smart she was. It was like she couldn't have both, they didn't want her to. They used to treat her very poorly in school, college, and other jobs. Libby was bound and determined to treat people with dignity and respect. When you add that to the mix, her colleagues felt even more threatened by her. Libby was used to backing herself up and double checking for mistakes. It actually helped her in her career. Noelle actually felt bad for her sister for what she's gone through. "So, you feel that if you date him they may go out of their way to ruin things?"

"Yes. I just don't need the added stress in my life. It's hard to keep a job when everyone wants to see you fall. I know that sounds paranoid, Noelle, but I'm serious. I hear them talk. They don't know I'm behind them or in the next room over. They say things, that want to see me fail. Not everyone, but there are so many out there that do, that I am often on guard. Don't get me wrong, I'm not complaining, I have friends and colleagues that respect me, but I just can't trust very many."

"I believe you." Noelle's had similar experiences in her life. Not nearly the way Libby has, but serious enough. She remembered times when people would pretend to be her friend and then gossip about her. It was ironic to Noelle that people always think it's better to be a different way, prettier, thinner, heavier, different color, different hair, the list goes on, but the reality is, gossip and bullying affects everyone equally. It doesn't discriminate. Libby understands that and keeps secrets, doesn't spread rumors, treats everyone fairly and with respect, doesn't judge based off anything physical, and for that she is treated terribly. Noelle was proud of her sister though because she handles it like a pro. It doesn't bring her down. For that reason, Libby is very successful. She's earned trust and respect.

Libby smiled. "So, why are you up so late?" she asked.

"I needed some water," Noelle said.

"You were worried about that globe, weren't you?"

"I just can't figure this one out," Noelle admitted.

"Sleep on it. Somehow we'll figure it out."

"Yeah, you're probably right. I just hate to come this far and not be able to solve it."

"Has anyone ever told you that you worry too much?" Libby asked with a grin.

"All the time."

"They're right, you know."

"Goodnight, Libs."

"Night."

Morning came before Noelle ever realized she was asleep. Realizing she must have slept hard, she jumped up to see what time it was. She was glad it was only 7:00. She was afraid that she had overslept again. Quickly, Noelle got up and hurried to go get dressed. She started breakfast just in time to see James heading out the door.

"Where are you going?" she asked, feeling a little disappointed.

"I'll be back. I have some calls to make. I'll be here in time to eat breakfast and help with the clue. An hour or so maybe?" James replied, leaving the house before she could ask any more questions.

Noelle shrugged. She finished making the omelets and then took it upon herself to wake up the Levi and Libby. They were already moving around anyway, so she didn't feel too bad disturbing them.

"Where's Daddy?" Levi asked, noticing James' absence.

"Oh honey, he had to go out for a minute. Don't worry, he'll be back," Noelle felt bad, thinking that having James back caused Levi confusion regarding his father.

"I'm not worried. I know Daddy will be here. He promised me, when he leaves, he will always come back. He pinky swore, Mom," Levi smiled and took a big drink of his orange juice.

Guilt flooded Noelle. She wished she could trust James the way Levi could. Then she reminded herself, she's the one that left him. He had to work. He always answered the phone, texted her, emailed her, and flew home as often as he could. He never not came back. That is until she left him. He never went after her and that fact bothered her more than anything else. Though she needed to remind herself sometimes, she left him. It was her choice. Noelle shook her head. Enough with the negativity. James would be back, he promised Levi. She decided she would save him an omelet after all.

Just when everyone was getting dressed, James walked through the door with a smile on his face. Noelle felt her tension ease as she saw him.

"You're back," she said.

"I told you I'd be right back," he was matter-of-fact.

"I saved you an omelet,"

"Thanks. I'm starving," James smiled and grabbed a plate.

Noelle felt there was something different about him. Something a little edgy or excited, maybe? She wasn't really sure. Regardless, she let him eat while she went into the other room to grab the globe. Not understanding the clue at all, she handed it to Libby. Libby looked at it and wound it up, just the same way Noelle did. She couldn't figure it out either.

"Where did they get married?" James asked, thinking that the wedding song may be a hint.

"In a church. It wasn't here," Noelle replied.

"What about their honeymoon?"

"Mackinac Island and then Tahquamenon Falls."

"Ha! Say that three times fast," James laughed. "I'm assuming that's not either, right?"

"Right."

"Do you recognize the place?"

"I feel like I do, but I can't place it."

"I was thinking the same," Libby agreed.

"We could ask around, see if anyone recognizes it," James suggested.

Noelle nodded. "We may have to. But once we're there, then what?" Noelle asked. "This clue is difficult."

"It's different, but I'm sure we'll figure it out."

Levi grabbed the snow globe. He shook it, spilling snow all over the building. He was watching as the snowflakes fell down, mesmerized by the tranquility of it.

"Levi, do that again," Libby said. "Watch, I saw something different when he shook it."

The adults gathered around Levi as she shook the snow globe. Sure enough, once the snow started to settle, inside the building just in front of the fire place was a rug. When the snow settled you couldn't really see the rug. On it, was a big red X.

"X marks the spot," James said, laughing. "Your mom was brilliant."

"Let's go see where this is at!" Noelle exclaimed feeling a little excited.

With a new sense of hope, the four of them got into the car in hopes of finding their mom's next clue. Noelle was trying to place that building, she knew she's seen it before, but where? She thought that she could always try going to the bank again, but then the last time the bank manager called the police on them and thank goodness James new the guy. Besides, not every building was in the train set. All streets were, but that train set was being added to regularly. It was a possibility they could see it, but it was also a possibility that they wouldn't. She assumed she could always ask strangers, but they already did that with finding Santa.

"It kind of looks like a lodge," Libby said out of nowhere.

"Let me see that again," James said. Grabbing the globe and turning it over in his hands, James started laughing.

"What's funny?" Noelle asked.

"Nothing. I know where this place is," James said. "Go down Main, take a left on Fourth, and then drive about three miles out. It's a wooded area, but not too far from town."

Libby gave him kind of a sideways glance and didn't say anything. James didn't seem to notice, or he ignored it.

"How do you know this place?" Noelle asked.

"I don't know, I guess my mom must have took us there as a kid," James replied, casually.

"You guys lived north about an hour," Noelle reminded him.

"Yeah, but we traveled. An hour isn't long," James shrugged.

Libby wasn't buying it. She stared at James, trying to figure out what he was hiding.

Noelle followed James' instructions and sure enough they pulled into a parking lot of the exact place in the snow globe. "Have we been here before?" Noelle asked Libby. "It just seems so familiar."

"I think so. I think we used to go skiing out here. Remember?"

"Yes! That's it. This place was beautiful until it had that fire. I heard they're trying to get it going again," Noelle remembered.

"Here, it looks empty, I'll go and check and see if anyone's here to let us in. You guys wait in the car," before they could object, James was already out the door and jogging toward the building.

"He's acting a little weird, isn't he?" Noelle asked.

"Nope, I don't think so," Libby lied.

Noelle shrugged. "Maybe it's just me."

Someone opened the door and James started to talk for a minute. He gave the person who answered the door a thumbs up, and ran back toward the car.

"They're here and they said we could go in," James smiled.

Walking toward the lodge Noelle remembered being a little girl and sledding down the big hills. When she was a little older, she was able to ski the other hills. Her mom took them there even after their dad passed. It was a calm spot to visit. Noelle always felt comfortable and at home there. They had several cabins in the back that they used to stay in once in a while. Noelle felt peaceful here, but wondered what made her mom put a clue at that particular place.

They walked inside and were immediately hit with the smell of burning wood. The fireplace that was in the clue was on and running. It smelled beautiful. Noelle imagined herself sitting on the hearth and warming her hands after a winter's day spent outside. It was relaxing and peaceful and instinctively she left the adults to go sit near the fire.

Libby looked around the room, remembering pieces of her childhood. If memory serves, this particular building was the gift shop and café. It was their favorite building out of the bunch. The rest were cabins, a health pavilion for emergencies, and things like that. This building was where the fun was at. Libby smiled as she could remember how alive it felt when she was young. She was sad to see it empty. A door shutting, took her out of her thoughts. She glanced up to witness a woman walking toward them and smiling.

"James, you decided to come back?" she said with a grin.

Libby glanced at Noelle to see if she noticed. Off in her own little world, Libby was relieved Noelle didn't hear. Libby looked at James expectantly.

James just shook his head and held out his hand. He shot the woman some kind of look and then said, "it's nice to meet you."

The woman cleared her throat and shook James' hand. Libby noticed the guy standing behind them that James was just talking to, was shaking his head, rapidly. The lady smiled and said, "I'm sorry, I thought you were someone else."

"That happens all the time," James laughed.

Libby stared.

"So, what can we help you with?" the woman asked, changing the subject and putting her business face on.

"Actually, this is kind of a funny story," James started to explain the clue scenario.

It was the man that seemed to understand. "You may take a look," was all he said.

The woman appeared to be very confused. As James lead the way, Libby noticed the man whispering something into the woman's ear. The lady nodded and smiled. All Libby could make out were the words, *'the irony'*. Aside from that she had no idea what was being said.

They joined Noelle who was sitting at the fireplace. She appeared to be totally at ease and perhaps even blissful. "I just love it here," she said.

Libby agreed. "I forgot all about this place, but now that I'm in it, I remember how much fun we had here."

"Wasn't there a café, bakery type thing over on that side? I think there was a gift store over here," Noelle stated.

"Yeah, I thought so too," Libby agreed.

James smiled. "My mom used to bring me and my brother here at least once a year. I can't believe they are selling it."

"What else could they do with it? Once it caught on fire..."

"I have a hunch they'll make a comeback," James replied.

"Mom, that's the rug with the X, isn't it?" Levi asked impatiently.

"I think it is," Noelle smiled looking at the old worn rug. It was almost an exact replica of the one in the snow globe that she was holding.

Levi started to walk on the rug trying to investigate, looking for a clue. He decided to lift the rug and check under there. Not seeing anything, he laid the rug back down and struggled to hide his disappointment.

"No clue!" he said.

"Don't be so quick to give up," James said. "Here, let's move the rug totally, and flip it upside down, just in case," he added.

Together, James and Levi grabbed each corner of the area rug and flipped it over and moved it out of the way. There was nothing where the rug was laying. James, rubbing the scruff on his face, tried to figure out what else the X could mean. Glancing at the rug, he realized why they didn't find the clue.

"Here it is!" James said. He walked over to the rug and sure enough, taped to the bottom of the rug was a small key.

Grabbing at the key, he glanced up at Noelle and Libby with confusion on his face. "Where do you think this goes to?" he asked.

Both girls shook their head. "We could ask, or we could explore," Libby stated.

"Let's just walk around for a moment and see if we find anything," James agreed.

The four of them looked around for anything that may take a key. They walked from room to room, looked under an empty case that used to hold a cash register, checked in the bathroom closet area, even tried the key in a paper towel holder, walked through the room past the people that were standing there, and into the kitchen area. Noelle smiled as she saw the stainless steel ovens.

"Do you know what you can do with that thing?" she said out loud.

Libby shook her head, "not a clue!" she said, honestly.

"Oh, Libs. There's just so much-"

"-We need to be finding the lock. The realtor told me that they had a showing for this place in a few minutes," James stated.

Libby looked at him funny. She wondered if he was telling the truth. She doubted it, but didn't mention anything.

"It's just amazing!" Noelle said as she grazed her hands over the nobs.

"One day, Noelle, you'll have your place," Libby said, though she was looking at James.

James didn't flinch. Libby may have noticed his jaw tightening, but she wasn't sure. Aside from that, no reaction. She wondered what that meant.

"One day," Noelle replied. Then walking away, she turned around and took one more look into the kitchen and nodded. "One day," she said again and then closed the door behind her.

"You guys look like you're looking for something. Can we offer any help?" The male realtor asked.

"We are looking for something that this key unlocks," James replied.

The realtor nodded his head. "The only place I could think of is the locker rooms, would you like to check them out, sir?" the guy asked.

James grinned. "Absolutely. You lead the way."

Libby swore she saw James wink at the guy. But then again, she was only looking at his side profile, perhaps he blinked. She wondered why she felt James was being so dishonest. It was uncomfortable for her because she's never had a hard time trusting her brother-in-law. What made it worse was that Noelle was slow to trust and seemed oblivious. She wondered if she was reading too much into that woman. She resolved that she probably was.

The man led them to a small room that was between the kitchen and the bathrooms. There were about 30 lockers in this room. Libby glanced around, noticing that some lockers were open, and some were closed. She was sure this is where they would find the next clue.

"Do you want to do the honors?" Noelle asked Libby.

Libby nodded. One by one she tried the key in the shut lockers. For each locker she tried the key one way and then flipped it upside down to try the other way, just to be sure. One after another the key didn't fit. With only a few lockers left, she could feel the disappointment start to swell up in her. Refusing to lose hope, she kept trying. With only two lockers left, Libby bit her bottom lip and shoved the key in the second to last locker. Much to her surprise the key fit. Libby turned the key and the locker popped right open. They were shocked to see a small tree sitting inside the locker.

Libby pulled the baby tree out and hanging from one of the branches was a note. Attached by a piece of purple thread that Noelle immediately recognized. It was the very thread she had on her sewing machine that she was using to make Libby's present. She remembered, that was the last thread that was on there from her mom stitching a purple wool jacket she had, before she decided to donate it to Goodwill. Grace refused to donate something that was no good. So, the coat had a small hole on the seam where the thread was cut and so she stitched the seam before donating the coat. Noelle remembered that like it was yesterday.

    Libby handed James the tree as she opened the note to read it. The only one that was written in her mother's writing, not typed, was this final clue.

MY ASHES ARE BURIED IN THE DIRT OF THIS TREE
PLEASE PLANT ME IN MY ABSOLUTE FAVORITE PLACE TO BE
WITH A BOOK THAT I LIKED TO READ
AWAY FROM PEOPLE THAT WERE FULL OF HATE AND GREED
MY SOUL IS UNITED WITH THE LORD THAT I LOVE
I'M FREE AS A BUTTERFLY OR THAT OF A DOVE
LEVI KNOWS THE EXACT PLACE I AM SURE
REMIND HIM THAT IT'S THE PLACE THAT IS QUIET AND PURE
REMEMBER THAT LOVE IS THE GREATEST THING
JAMES YOU KNOW IT'S TIME TO GIVE NOELLE BACK HER RING
LIBBY DON'T BE AFRAID TO DATE
I REALLY THINK YOU HAVE A GOOD CHANCE WITH NATE
LEVI THIS WAS FUN AND GRANNY LOVES YOU
TAKE CARE OF YOUR MOTHER SHE LOVES YOU TOO
RICHARD HAS A GLOBE I MADE FOR EACH OF YOU
THIS IS THE FINAL CHRISTMAS CLUE
MY GIFT TO YOU ALL WAS A CLEVER ONE
TOGETHER WE GOT TO HAVE SOME CHRISTMAS FUN

Libby started to read it, but she couldn't finish. Her hand started to shake as her eyes welled up. Noelle was surprised. She looked at James, because if Libby couldn't read it, there was no way that Noelle could. James, understanding, nodded and took the note. Slowly, carefully, he read the words that their mother had wrote. Even his voice quivered a little, but he continued to read. When the note was finished, he looked at Noelle and Libby and he stretched out both of his arms, pulling them both in close to him. Together, the three of them stood. A family.

It was Levi to break the lulling sobs of his mother. "Granny wants us to plant the tree in her backyard by the creek. She wants the Bible to go with her. She has a tiny one that she carried with her everywhere she went. She told me her favorite thing to do was watch the sun go down, while she drank her lemon water, by the creek. She called that her peaceful place."

Noelle nodded as she wiped the tears from her face.

"Sounds about right, buddy," she said.

"One time, granny thought there was a crocodile in the creek. She kept saying, 'Levi there can't be a crocodile in Michigan. Not an alligator either,' she stared and stared and she made me stand behind her as she walked up the creek with a giant stick. You know what it was, Mom?"

"What's that bud?"

"It was a log that had a chipmunk on it. She thought that was funny. She made me promise not to tell you, because you would say she was senile!" Levi laughed. "It was so funny."

Noelle started laughing. Grace would always say, *"I'm not going senile, I just can't see that well."* She looked at her son, feeling overcome with emotion. She was grateful he was there with them. Together, they thanked the realtor, who had given them a moment, and they took the baby tree out to the car.

"Tomorrow is Christmas Eve. Should we plant it then? Mom always liked Christmas Eve better than Christmas Day," Libby reminded them.

Noelle nodded. "I do think we should go see Richard. The goal was to have this done before Christmas and I bet he's closed on Christmas Eve."

"Let's have lunch and cool down and then we can go there," Libby agreed.

James nodded. "Can you give me just a second, I have to use the phone. I will meet you guys in the car?"

Noelle nodded. Libby looked at him suspiciously but didn't say anything. If she wasn't mistaken, she could have sworn that James left his cell phone in the car. She walked out with Noelle and Levi, and volunteered to make sure Levi was buckled up. She did this purposefully, so she didn't alert Noelle, especially if she were to notice his phone sitting there. She checked the backseat and just as she suspected James' phone was sitting right next to Levi's booster seat. Quietly she grabbed his phone and shoved it into her pocket.

A few moments later, James was standing in the doorway and shook the realtor's hand. The realtor smacked him on the shoulder, the two shared a laugh and James nodded at him. He then shoved his hands in his pockets and ran toward the car.

"Sorry about that," he said. "Let's get some food," he offered no explanation or anything. Libby bore a hole at him. James avoided her eyes.

Before long, they pulled into a restaurant and sat down to eat. None of them were really talkative. They sat pretty much sat in silence as they ate their food. Even Levi was unusually quiet. Suddenly, Libby came to a realization and stopped eating, a look of confusion on her face.

"What?" Noelle asked.

"How did Mom know about Nate?" she asked.

"I have no idea. Call Nate and ask him," Noelle replied.

"I feel sick. How could she have possibly known?"

"Libby, Christmas magic, I guess. How did the clues stay where they were at for 7 months and not move? How did she know people would be there, that something didn't get changed or anything like that? She had everything worked out perfectly to the day. How did any of this happen, really? The whole thing was magic. Mom was amazing, but there had to be a little something extra mixed in the combination."

"Your mom was something else," James agreed. "She was special."

Quietly, they finished eating. All of them thinking about how in the world Grace pulled this whole thing off. Quietly, with the tree in tow, they walked into the lawyer's office.

"How are you guys doing?" he asked.

"Fine, thank you." Noelle held up the tree with the final clue on it. "We finished the clues and the last one told us to come back here," Noelle stated.

"That was quite the journey wasn't it?" Richard asked. "I had no idea if she would be able to pull it off, but it looks like she did."

"How did she do it?" Noelle asked.

"Seriously, no idea. Your mom was a remarkable lady," Richard shrugged.

"So, you have something for us?" Libby asked.

"I do. Please sign the form below and I will grab the gifts," Richard handed them a form to sign. Each person, including Levi, passed the paper and the pen around and each person signed it. Richard then stood up and walked into a different room. He came back holding a gift bag, delicately wrapped, for each person.

"We can take these home and put them under the tree," Noelle said.

"Actually, I can't have you do that. I need you to open them now," Richard informed her. "Your mother had strict rules."

Noelle nodded. She looked at her package apprehensively. She was hesitant on whether or not she wanted to experience anything else emotional on this day.

"I'll go first," James said. He opened the gift and pulled out a snow globe. It had a miniature version of him reading a book on the edge of Levi's bed. Noelle was standing in the doorway. The details of each person in the globe were extravagant. He couldn't believe the likeness of everyone, it was amazing. Inscribed on the bottom was *'a blessed father and husband.'*

"I'll do mine next," Libby stated. She tore into the paper and pulled out her snow globe. She was staring at herself with a stethoscope around her neck. She had a smile on her face and her mother painted a wedding ring on her left hand. Libby wondered who the husband was. She looked happy and beautiful. Inscribed on the bottom was, *'forever loved and never alone.'* Libby smiled and shook her head. Her mother was perfect.

Levi opened his. His globe showed a little boy playing in the snow, his brown curls sticking out of his hat, there was a snowman toward the back and a puppy by his side. Levi kind of gave the globe a funny look.

"I don't have a dog," he said. He read the bottom and it said, *"dreams do come true."* Richard walked over to Levi and handed him a leash and a collar.

"I'm going to miss this little fella," Richard said. He went around the back of the room and handed Levi a box. There was a baby lab sitting in the box. He looked exactly like a miniature version of the one in the snow globe.

"Yes! Yes! I've always wanted a puppy!" Levi shouted as he picked up the dog and held it close to him. "Is it a boy or a girl?" he asked.

"It's a girl."

"Her name is Angel. I'm going to name her Angel. I think my grandma Grace would like that!" Levi grabbed Angel and immediately strapped the collar onto her. Tears of joy were sliding down his cheeks. "I love you, Angel!" he said.

Everyone looked at Noelle expectantly. She opened her package. Inside her snow globe was Noelle holding onto Levi's hand. Next to her was James. There was a little girl holding onto his hand. They were walking toward a building. The lodge? The inscription said, *'a beloved mother and wife and the world's greatest chef.'*

"I have none of this," Noelle said, confused.

"You don't now, you never know what the future brings," James said, grabbing her hand.

Richard interrupted. "Noelle, Libby. Your mother has left you another life insurance policy," he handed each girl a check. "Libby, it was requested that yours pays for the rest of your medical school and whatever bills you accumulate while you go," he handed the check to Libby.

"Noelle, yours was specified for repairs for the house or to help you afford a new one. She wanted you to be secure in housing while you work on starting a restaurant. She wanted me to tell you not to worry if you decide to move. She expects it some time, due to you probably having more children." Richard handed her a check.

Noelle wiped her face. This was just too much for her. "This makes no sense," Noelle said out loud.

"Actually, Noelle it doesn't sound too far off," Libby replied. "I'm sorry, but it's not that crazy."

Noelle looked at her.

"If that's the case, you know you're getting married, right?" she said.

"Hopefully, one day I will. Until then, I can laugh at what mom's plans were for me, until they come true."

"Another baby? A restaurant? A bigger home? What's wrong with the house I have? Mom's house. None of this stuff seems feasible to me. I don't have the ability to do any of this. I am barely making it now. I mean the bills are paid, but I have to watch what I spend. I can't afford to just plan my future like this," reluctantly she took the check from the lawyer and put it in her purse.

Libby and James glanced at each other, both of them able to see more clearly than what Noelle could. Richard looked at all of them and smiled. "Your mother also started an account at the credit union for Levi's college fund. The information for said account is on this paper," he handed Noelle another paper with account information on it.

Libby thanked Richard.

"You've been very helpful to our family. Thank you for making my mom's dreams come true," Libby said to him.

"It's been my pleasure!" Richard replied.

After shaking everyone's hand, Richard led them out the door, "If any of you need anything at all, please feel free to contact me. It was both, a blessing and an honor to work with Grace," he said.

They thanked him and walked away. Silently they went back to Noelle's house. That night, Noelle didn't really feel like cooking, so she whipped up some hamburgers really quick and served them with some chips. Everyone ate, but it was a quiet meal. In the air was a combination of sadness but also confusion, tied in with a little bit of hope. The following day was Christmas

Eve. Noelle knew she was going to have to get out of this funk and bake some cookies if there's ever going to be any. Taking a deep breath she put some Christmas music on and got to work.

She would have asked Levi to help her, but he was occupied on the floor with Angel. Which reminded her, now that they have a dog, they're going to need to buy dog food and things. Noelle's mother had dog dishes and a few toys in the box that Angel came in. However, that happened, Noelle will never know, the dog was just six weeks old. How could that have possibly been planned? Inside the box was a small bag of food, but that would only last a small while. Noelle jotted down puppy chow on the list that was stuck to her fridge.

Noelle started to beat some batter, adding ingredients as she went. She never once looked at a recipe. She was singing along quietly when James walked into the kitchen. He watched her with her hair tied up in a loose bun on top of her head, eyes closed, adding a pinch of this and a dash of that. She never even had to look at the ingredients she was adding, she just knew. She was dancing with the bowl in her hands, totally at peace with what she was doing. James shook his head in awe. She was radiant.

A few moments later, Libby walked into the room. She stood by James and then nodded for him to follow her out of the room. He obeyed, stealing a glance at Noelle before he left.

"What is it?" he asked.

"I have your phone. You left it in the car earlier when you lied to Noelle and said you were on your phone. I guess I saved you from getting caught. Mind explaining what's going on?" Libby was direct but also kind.

"Thanks for grabbing it. Libby, this day has been insane. I promise you everything is good. I'll fill you in on Christmas. I have a few details to iron out. Do you think you can vouch for me if

Noelle gets suspicious?" he asked, not eluding to what he was doing at all.

"Only if you're not hurting my sister," she stated.

"I promise. Thank you!" he said. "Now I need to get back in there and try to convince Noelle not to divorce me," James smiled. "Do you think I have a chance?"

"If you're honest with her, absolutely. She's head over heels in love with you."

"I hope so. Wish me luck," James said.

"Good luck."

James walked into the kitchen. He grinned as Noelle was plopping batter onto a cookie sheet. It already smelled good in the room, he couldn't wait to try one of the cookies she was baking. He took a deep breath, exhaled slowly and hoped for the best.

"My hope is that you will stay married to me. My dream is that we have more children, together. My preference is a big family, but I will keep a small family if you're opposed to a big one. I also dream that I can live each day making you the happiest woman on earth. What I can't live without is you. Noelle, I will never once regret staying here as long as you're by my side. That's my list."

Noelle looked at him. Her heart overflowed with joy. She couldn't deny it any longer. More than anything, she wanted her husband back. She wasn't sure why she fought it so hard to begin with. Perhaps fear does that to a person. She looked at him with a smile on her face and said, "I want a big family too."

James grabbed ahold of her and sat her on the countertop. He reached into his pocket and pulled out a ring. "Noelle, I bought you a ring to go with your wedding ring. I don't want it to replace it. I just want to add another section to it. A section that represents the growth of our love and how even through the hard times, we grow together. A ring that represents our future and what it holds. I love you, Noelle. I have yesterday, I do today, and I will tomorrow. I truly love you."

Noelle's hands were shaking as James started to place the ring on her finger. After a moment he started to laugh. "You still wear your wedding ring," he said.

"I only took it off the day you came to town," she admitted.

James started to laugh. "I took mine off that day too." He raised his left hand, his wedding band was already back in place where it belonged.

The two started to laugh when the oven dinged. "I have to pull the cookies out of the oven. I don't want to burn them."

"There's got to be a first for everything," James said as he met her mouth with his.

Noelle giggled, happily holding onto her guy, regardless of the cookies.

Chapter Thirteen
Christmas Celebrations

Noelle got up early that morning. It was not even 6:30 yet. Everyone was still sleeping as she turned the oven on. She didn't mind that they were sleeping, she turned the Christmas music on too and started to cook. She slept like a baby that night and felt like she was in an exceptionally good mood. She wanted to get a head start on her Christmas cooking, since they were going to be eating as a family and had a guest coming over. She really hoped that Libby and Nate would hit it off, she could see them being a great relationship.

She put the pies in the oven and then scrambled some eggs for breakfast. A simple breakfast of eggs and toast would have to suffice, she had too much to do that day. Before long, the smell of warm apple pie filled the house up. Just about the time she was to pull the pie out of the oven, everyone else woke up.

She turned to set the dishes at the table when she stepped in something and yelled. "Levi, you come clean up after this dog."

Libby came in laughing at Noelle until she stepped in something too. "Gross!" she yelled. "Levi this dog went all over the place!"

Levi came running through the house carrying his puppy. "I forgot dogs have to go outside to use the bathroom," he said. Levi put Angel on the leash and took her outside. He was out for about five minutes before he came back in. As soon as he did, Angel peed on the floor.

"Levi!"

James came around the corner. He grabbed some sanitary wipes and crated the dog. Together, he and Levi got to work cleaning up the messes while Libby showered and Noelle finished cooking. James was grinning the entire time. Noelle kind of gave him a funny look.

James shrugged. "This is what I always pictured my life to be like," he said smiling. "This is perfect."

Noelle laughed and shook her head. "Have you told Levi yet?" she asked him.

"I didn't know if you would want me to, or if you wanted to," he admitted.

"You can tell him, he'll be thrilled."

"I'll have him help me dig the hole for the tree. I'll tell him then, man to man."

Noelle smiled. She hated the idea of the tree, but she knew it was what her mother wanted. It had to get done. After breakfast, Noelle explained to everyone that she had cooking to do all day. Libby explained that she still had shopping to do, so she would be in and out. Levi and James had to dig the hole. Libby decided to wait until they planted the tree to finish her things up.

About an hour later, James said it was time. Noelle and Libby glanced at each other and each took a deep breath. Libby grabbed the tree and the four of them walked outside to their mother's peaceful place, facing the creek. They each said their good-byes and placed the tree inside the ground. It was solemn and quiet. James thought it was strange that the ground was still able to be dug. He expected it to be more frozen than what it was. Carefully, he tied a plastic tarp around the tree and anchored the tree down. Levi helped pour the dirt onto the tree and stopped it in. Noelle and Libby watched in peace, both sad, but also content. This was what their mother wanted.

After a day of cooking, shopping, and getting ready for Christmas, everyone was ready to go to bed that night. James took it upon himself to lay with Levi, so Noelle could bring the gifts into the living room and place them under the tree.

"Daddy, I'm glad you're here for Christmas this year," Levi said.

"Oh, I forgot to tell you. Daddy's staying here with you guys," James told him.

"You mean, for forever?"

"For forever."

"What about Japan?"

"I don't work there anymore."

"Where do you work?"

"Can you keep a secret?"

"Yup."

"I'm going to work with your momma."

"Doing what?"

"You'll see."

"Daddy, mommy's globe had a sister in it. Instead, can you make it be a brother?"

"I don't know Buddy, we'll just have to wait and see what happens."

"Sisters whine too much. Angel whines and whimpers a lot."

"Boys cry and whine too."

"Oh. Well, goodnight daddy."

"Goodnight, son."

James waited until Levi was asleep before he left the bedroom and joined Noelle. He looked at the tree and smiled. "I haven't seen a Christmas like this since I was a kid," he stated.

"Did you want to bring your gifts in?" Noelle asked.

"My gifts are already under the tree," James explained.

"Oh. I'm surprised. You didn't get Levi the bike?"

"No. I respected your wishes. I'm not going to trump what you got him. I think the scooter is a great gift."

Noelle smiled.

"You're a good man, James," she said.

"That's because I have a good woman by my side."

Noelle nodded. "I'm going to bed," she said, yawning.

"Sleep well, Noelle. I'm going to sit here for a while."

Noelle nodded and went to bed.

Noelle opened her eyes to see the sun peaking into her room. It was Christmas. She stretched and yawned, feeling the effects of cooking the day before. Her muscles were tight, her body sore, and she was already ready to start again. She wanted this day to be perfect. She jumped out of bed and started breakfast. Since Libby stayed at her house that night, Noelle wasn't sure if she was going to be present for breakfast or not. She decided to cook enough, just in case.

As soon as breakfast was over, Noelle heard the front door open. It was Libby.

"Aunt Libby, we're going to be opening presents!" Levi exclaimed, excitedly.

"Do you want breakfast?" Noelle asked.

"I'd love some," she yawned.

Noelle looked at her sister, confused. She didn't seem as upbeat as normal. "You okay?"

"Yeah, I just didn't sleep a wink last night."

"How come?"

"I don't know. I kept wondering what it would be like with Nate here. What if he doesn't like me?"

"Libby, you're nervous! I've never seen you nervous over a guy before!"

Libby shrugged as she cut into her pancake. She ate a few bites and then threw the rest in the garbage. "I can't eat."

"You're in love!" Noelle exclaimed, excitedly. "That's what it is!"

Libby blushed. "No, I'm not. I barely even know the guy."

"Libs, it's obvious," Noelle started to laugh.

"He's a lucky guy," James said smiling. "Let's open presents."

The girls followed James into the living room. Noelle was surprised to see a trainset going around the Christmas tree. She smiled as she knew what inspired that gift. The way Levi was so infatuated with the train at the bank, James took it upon himself to get him one. The train drove around the track and the way James had it set up, it drove under a tunnel of gifts. Levi thought it was amazing.

Levi opened his presents. When he got to his scooter, he let out a big screech. "This is the best Christmas ever!" he yelled. Levi grabbed his scooter and started riding it through the house. "Can I take it outside?" he asked.

"You can in a bit," Noelle replied.

Libby opened her gift. Noelle showed her how the she took all of their mom's old shirts that she wore for painting and things and cut them, using the material for quilting pillows. Libby loved them. Noelle had given her a total of five. When she laid them out each pillow had a letter on it to spell, 'Grace'. Libby couldn't believe how Noelle could do that in such a short amount of time. When it came to artistic talent, Noelle definitely had their mom's genes.

Libby handed Noelle a gift. She opened it up to see a CD sitting in there. "It's mom and dad's wedding song and then yours and James wedding song. Then I added yours and Levi's song, the one you always sang to him when he was a baby. Then I took the liberty of adding a new lullaby on there, you know, just in case," Libby explained.

Noelle put the CD into the player. Soon the music started to play and Noelle couldn't believe her ears. "Wait, Libs, you sang these?"

"Yeah. It's my voice. I sang each one for you to have."

"This is beautiful! I love it!"

"Thank you," Libby replied.

"My goodness, Libby, you sound professional!"

Libby smiled and shrugged. She wished she were a professional. That was her dream.

There was a knock on the door. Libby's face dropped. "Shut the CD off," she whispered. It was too late, Levi already opened the door.

"Hi. I hope I'm not too early, I just figured I'd stop by and help out if anyone needed help," Nate said.

James walked up to him and shook his hand. He then quietly said something to Nate. Nate looked at him funny and shook his head. James nodded. Nate stood in the door, quiet for a second. He then looked at James and said, "really?"

James nodded.

"Libby your voice is spectacular!" Nate said.

Libby blushed. "Thank you."

"I can't believe that's you."

Libby nodded.

They all stood there listening to Libby's voice come across the speakers. Each note sung in a perfect tune, to her own melody, making the song hers. She sounded better than most professionals. Libby smiled and then said, "can we turn it off now?"

Noelle turned it off and thanked Libby for the amazing gift. Libby nodded, shyly.

"So, you're a doctor?" Noelle asked.

"Yes, a pediatrician," Nate replied.

"Wow, Libby, it looks to me like he's met the criteria on your list," Noelle grinned at the horror on Libby's face.

Once dinner was over, James approached Noelle. "Hey, I have one last present for you," he said.

Noelle smiled. "Another one?"

James nodded. He got on one knee and presented her with a black velvet box. "Noelle Miller, will you give me the honor of cooking for me forever?"

Noelle looked at him funny. James opened the box. Inside was a key. Libby smiled. She knew exactly what this was about. Noelle was confused.

"What's this?" she asked.

"Well, if you say yes, it's the key to your restaurant."

Noelle was dumbfounded.

"It's at the lodge isn't it?" Libby asked, laughing.

James looked at her and smiled. "I almost got sick when the clue took us there. I had already bought it beforehand. That's where I was going when I had to take care of things," he admitted.

"The lodge? You bought me the lodge? James how can we afford this?"

"Noelle, no worries. It's all taken care of. By the way, I retired. No more Tokyo ever again."

Noelle started to tear up. "Are you serious?"

"It's all yours."

"James, how could I ever thank you?"

"By loving me every day."

"I already do."

James pulled Noelle into his arms and kissed her. "I will love you forever," he said.

"I will love you even longer."

Libby looked at Nate and smiled. He reached over and grabbed her hand. "You're beautiful," he said.

"Nate, how did my mom know you?" Libby asked.

"What do you mean?" Nate asked, confused.

"She put you in the clue."

"Who was your mother?"

"Grace. Grace White."

"Oh! I know Grace. She interviewed me and then offered me the job at the hospital," Nate said.

"How did she know I'd meet you?" Libby asked.

"I don't know. She's the one that told me about the ball. She said if I get lonely, that's a great place to meet people. That's all."

"It was just Christmas magic," Libby said, smiling.

"Christmas magic," Noelle agreed.

Epilogue
One Year Later

Noelle stood in the backyard looking at the tree that they planted for their mother. The snowflakes were coming down steadily. Noelle pulled the sweater tight around her. She loved to go sit by that tree and talk to her mom. As she walked closer to the baby tree, Noelle was shocked to see that the apple blossoms were in bloom.

"Impossible," she said to herself. She shook her head as she sat down on the bench that James built for her, in her mom's favorite place.

"Well, Nate's proposing to Libby. They're perfect together, but you already knew." Noelle smiled. "Mom, how did you know everything?" she sat there listening to the silence. A moment later James joined her. He sat next to her and wrapped his arms around her waist, resting them on her belly.

"Your mom was amazing," James said. "She knew it would be a girl."

"I decided to name her Grace."

James nodded. "It's perfect."

Noelle nodded. "The restaurant, Nate and Libby, Levi's dog, me and you, the baby, it's like she knew everything. How can that happen?"

James smiled at her and said, "Christmas magic."

Noelle laughed. "Let's get inside and watch Nate propose to my sister."

"Noelle, how is the tree in bloom in the middle of December? Apple trees don't even bloom until they're around six," James asked confused.

"You already know. It's *Christmas magic.*"

A note from the author:

Thanks for reading my story. If you enjoyed this book as much as I enjoyed writing it, please do me a favor and leave a review on Amazon or on goodreads and tell your friends. Reviews help independent authors like me to not only gain more readers but also grow in our craft. We value honest feedback almost as much as we value our fans. As always, thank you and God bless!

-Christina Cooper

Feel free to reach out at:

christina@christinacooperunpublished.com

Manufactured by Amazon.ca
Bolton, ON